Fenella-Jane Miller lives in an ancient cottage in acres of Essex woodland near Colchester with her husband, a border collie, an arthritic cat and numerous chickens. She worked as a teacher, restaurateur and hotelier before becoming a full-time writer. She has two grown-up children and two grandchildren.

THE MÉSALLIANCE

Lady Allegra Humphry, being at the top of the aristocratic tree, has no time for *cits* — suitors from the merchant class. But she and her brother, Richard, the Earl of Witherton, must make compromises if they are to retain their position in society. Self-made millionaire Silas Tremayne now owns Allegra's ancestral home, and is determined to own her as well. Rejected by the *haut ton*, Silas plans to ensure both he and his daughter, Demelza, will be welcome in the best drawing-rooms. Marriage is the answer! But there are people against the union, and those who are prepared to commit murder to stop it . . .

Books by Fenella-Jane Miller
Published by The House of Ulverscroft:

THE UNCONVENTIONAL MISS WALTERS
A SUITABLE HUSBAND
A DISSEMBLER

FENELLA-JANE MILLER

THE MÉSALLIANCE

Complete and Unabridged

ULVERSCROFT
Leicester

First published in Great Britain in 2007 by
Robert Hale Limited
London

First Large Print Edition
published 2008
by arrangement with
Robert Hale Limited
London

British Library CIP Data

Miller, Fenella-Jane
   The mésalliance.—Large print ed.—
   Ulverscroft large print series: historical romance
   1. Aristocracy (Social class)—Fiction 2. Millionaires
   —Fiction 3. Romantic suspense novels
   4. Large type books
   I. Title
   823.9′2 [F]

   ISBN 978–1–84782–062–4

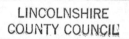
Published by
F. A. Thorpe (Publishing)
Anstey, Leicestershire

Set by Words & Graphics Ltd.
Anstey, Leicestershire
Printed and bound in Great Britain by
T. J. International Ltd., Padstow, Cornwall

This book is printed on acid-free paper

For my brother Tony, the best brother any sister could have, and for his wife Susan, for her help and encouragement.

Acknowledgements

I would like to thank Miss Phyllis Hendy, the St Osyth village historian, for her help with my research. She kindly allowed me to see the documents in the Parish Museum and arranged for me to accompany her on a tour of St Osyth Priory.

I would also like to thank Mr John Sergeant, the owner of St Osyth Priory, for allowing me to use his wonderful home as the setting for this book.

PROLOGUE

July 1811

The man in the study at St Osyth's Priory opened the carved box and removed the duelling pistol. He checked it was primed and then slowly raised it to his right temple and pulled the trigger. He slumped lifeless across the desk and the blood pooled under his shattered face.

Lady Allegra Humphry was on the way back from her evening stroll in the inner courtyard when she heard the shot. Her eyes widened, she spun, and picking up her skirts, ran towards the open window, dreading what she might find.

Her screams of anguish echoed around the garden, alerting Thomas Smith, the head coachman, who had been standing outside the harness-room. He was the first to arrive at her side. A man of medium height, he was forced to crane his head to see past Lady Allegra. Grim faced, he reached up and pushed the window shut.

'Come away, my lady, there is nothing you can do.'

She was no longer screaming but the silence was worse. Her blue eyes were huge, her face bloodless. Thomas decided protocol would, this once, have to be ignored, and he slipped his arm around her waist, supporting her easily. A small group of outside staff stood gaping at the sight of their young mistress cradled in the arms of the head coachman.

'Ben, run inside and fetch Miss Murrell and Mrs Wright. Bill, you get Mr Digby; he was working in the estate office earlier, try there first.' Thomas scowled at the other three. 'Get back to your duties; this has naught to do with you.' Touching their caps, they backed away. They knew when they were not wanted.

He heard the sound of approaching footsteps and two women appeared from around the corner. Miss Murrell, Lady Allegra's companion, arrived first.

'Here, Thomas, let me take her ladyship from you.'

'Yes, madam.' He hesitated, not sure if either Miss Murrell, or the housekeeper, knew what had caused her ladyship's collapse. Should he be the first to break the news?

Mrs Wright, her face red, her plump cheeks glistening, also placed her arm around Allegra's waist. He knew he was redundant.

'Come along, my dear, One foot in front of the other; we will soon have you safe in your bed,' Miss Murrell crooned.

'It's the ague; this damp weather we have been having makes it worse,' Mrs Wright said.

Miss Murrell noticed Thomas hovering beside them. 'Off you go now. Lady Allegra does not need you any more.'

'She's not poorly, Miss Murrell, she's had a mortal bad shock.' Both women froze, waiting to hear the rest, the slender form hanging, almost comatose, between them. 'His Lordship — he's gone and killed himself. Her ladyship must have heard the shot and she saw him in the study.'

Miss Murrell recovered first. 'How dreadful! It's no wonder Lady Allegra is so shocked. We must deal with things as they stand.' She nodded briskly to the housekeeper, now almost as pale as their charge and, arms linked, the two middle-aged ladies half carried Allegra inside.

Mr Digby, the estate manager, when informed of the situation understood at once what had to be done. 'Thomas, did anyone apart from yourself see into the study?'

'No, sir, I stood in front. All they saw was me holding her ladyship. That was shock enough, I can tell you.'

'Excellent. Tell the rest of the staff that his

lordship collapsed at his desk. We can count on Miss Murrell and Mrs Wright to remain silent. No one must ever suspect the truth, you do understand that?'

'I do, sir. Will I go to London and fetch back Lord Richard? I mean, Lord Witherton?'

'Yes, travel post.' Mr Digby rummaged in the pocket of his tweed jacket and extracted a small cloth purse. 'There is more than enough here. I'll have a change of horses waiting at Chelmsford. His lordship will no doubt wish to drive himself back.'

★　★　★

Allegra wanted to explain, to tell Miss Murrell what she had seen, but the words wouldn't form in her mouth.

'Come along, my dear, into bed with you. I have something here to help you sleep. Things will seem better in the morning.'

Obediently she opened her mouth and swallowed the thick syrup. She forced her eyelids to stay up, knowing that the image of her beloved father, his gentle features obliterated by the bullet, would return to haunt her as soon as she let them fall.

'Close your eyes, my dear. I promise, you will not have nightmares. The poppy syrup will ensure you have a peaceful, dreamless sleep.'

Her brother returned and the funeral of the Earl of Witherton took place less than six months after a similar service for the countess. The staff and village believed that shock and grief, caused by his wife's death, had caused an apoplexy. His suicide had been well disguised.

1

April 1812

Richard looked across at his sister. 'Are you sure you wish to go ahead with the dinner party this evening, you look fagged to death.'

Lady Allegra stiffened. 'Thank you, Richard, it is always good to know one looks one's best.'

'Do not fly up into the boughs, Allegra, I am expressing my concern. You have dark circles under your eyes, that is all, but you look, as always, truly lovely. And that new gown you have on is most flattering.'

She relaxed a little. 'Oh, do you like it? I had this cambric made up specially for today. The opals you gave me for our last name day reflect the colour admirably.' She glanced down at her ensemble. 'Do you think it is too soon to be wearing lavender?'

'Absolutely not! Good God, you were in black for Mama for six months before Papa died. Fifteen months is more than long enough to be walking around like a crow.'

Allegra was not impressed. 'The fact that you are my twin does not give you leave to insult me, Richard. So far this morning you have told me I look 'fagged to death' and that I look like a crow.'

Richard grinned, unrepentant. 'But I also said you look lovely and that I like your new gown.' His smile faded. 'Are you still not sleeping, Allegra?'

She changed the subject. 'How are you intending to spend the day, Richard?'

He sauntered across to the mullioned window through which the pale April sunlight filtered. 'Gideon and I are riding to Colchester this morning. Do you wish to accompany us?'

Allegra shook her head. The attentions of Captain Gideon Pledger, an old schoolfriend of her brother's, were becoming decidedly irksome. 'If Captain Pledger is well enough to complete a ride of almost thirty miles why has he not returned to his regiment in Spain?'

'It is his shoulder. It is still festering and he cannot return until the wound is quite healed.'

Her mouth pursed in disgust. 'Pray, spare me the details, Richard. Well, let us hope he soon recovers and is able to leave here. His visit has been over long already.'

'He is a pleasant fellow, Allegra. And he is a good friend to me.' He saw her fine eyebrows arch and grinned. 'I know — he is a trifle wild

— but there is no real harm in him. And I swear rusticating down here since last July would have become unbearable without him at the Priory to keep me company these past two months.'

She had discussed the captain quite long enough. 'I shall see you tonight, Richard. I trust that you will be ready in time to greet our guests. Remember we are celebrating a quarter-century together; it is a significant occasion.'

'Do not fuss, Sister, we will be back in good time.'

She watched him stride out, not a care in the world, his shoulders unbowed by estate business or household concerns. Assuming the title had not changed him one iota. He had merely continued his heedless existence, gambling, whoring, and driving *entre à terre* all over the Essex countryside instead of London and its environs.

He was her twin, and she loved him dearly, but she wished he would take more interest in their affairs. She frowned. It was passing strange that the lawyers had not come to visit since that horrible day last July. She shuddered as she recalled it.

As if it had not been bad enough to lose her father in such a beastly way, to discover later that she had been seen in the arms of her coachman, however innocent the occasion, had added to her distress. She was no longer comfortable with him and if Ned, the under-coachman, was not available, she stayed at home.

A polite tap on the door heralded the arrival of her companion, and former governess, Miss Grace Murrell. 'Come in, Miss Murrell. I was about to ring for coffee, would you care to join me?'

'I will, thank you. I have the menu for tonight; do you wish to see it, my dear?'

'No, I am sure you have arranged it all perfectly. I am still unconvinced that holding a party, however small, is not unseemly when we are still in half mourning.'

'Nonsense, my love. We could not allow such an important anniversary to pass unremarked. And you have only invited close friends, after all.'

Allegra wrinkled her elegant nose. 'I would hardly call Lady Arabella Grierson and her new husband, intimates, Miss Murrell. Nor young Edward Grierson and his feather-brained sister Emily.'

'They are, my dear girl, the only acquaintances you have down here. I have always said you are far too particular. And Lady Arabella is of equal rank to you; her father is an earl.'

Allegra shrugged. 'But he is only the fifth

earl; they do not trace their line back to Edward the Confessor, as we do.'

'That's as may be, my love. As you know, I have always thought your refusing to even consider any man below the rank of duke has left . . . ' She paused, unwilling to say what she felt.

'Do go on, Miss Murrell. Has left me at my last prayers? A spinster with five and twenty years in her dish and no prospects of a match?'

Miss Murrell flushed. Much as she loved her charge she did sometimes wish she was a little less sharp. 'I am certain that, had your dear mother not been so ill and you had been able to have a third season, you would have found someone who suited you. You are a lovely young woman, with an impeccable pedigree. You should be spoilt for choice.'

Allegra stared critically at her reflection in the gilt glass hanging over the mantel. 'I agree that my eyes are unusual, periwinkle-blue is not a common colour, but my hair is too pale to be fashionable and I do not have the requisite ringlets. Also I consider I am too thin and too tall.' Then she smiled and her pale oval face was transformed. On the rare occasions she did so even the most critical of observers could not have failed to label her a diamond of the first water.

'I apologize for being so abrupt. I do not mean to be but I am so tired all the time. I do not believe I have had a natural night's rest since . . . since last July. As soon as my eyes close I am visited by the most horrible nightmares.' She paused, knowing what her mentor was thinking. 'I know, I should not resort to laudanum, but it is the only rest I get. One cannot survive without sleep.'

'It is addictive. It should be used only in extreme circumstances. I do not consider lack of sleep, Lady Allegra, to be such a one.'

Allegra drew breath to deliver a terse reply but was prevented by a sharp knock on the drawing-room door. She ignored it, knowing that Miss Murrell would deal with the interruption.

Yardley, the elderly butler, stepped in.

'Forgive me, your ladyship, but there are two gentlemen here to see you and his lordship.' He held out the heavily embossed silver salver on which rested a thick cream rectangle. Allegra removed it with distaste. She had no wish to see anyone and especially not two unknown gentlemen.

She scanned the card and her nostrils flared. 'Lord Witherton will not be back until late afternoon. Yardley, have Mr Evans and his companion, placed in the small drawing-room. Make sure they have all they require and explain the circumstances. If they do not care to wait then they must return another day.'

The butler bowed and walked backwards from the room. As soon as they were alone she turned to Miss Murrell, her face flushed.

'I believe it is good news, Miss Murrell; I remember Papa telling Richard and me, when we achieved our majority, that we would receive a substantial sum on this particular name day.' She clapped her hands and whirled like a schoolgirl, sending her skirt swirling indecorously. 'I am to be an independent woman. I shall no longer be obliged to go cap in hand for pin money to Richard, or anyone else. I think as soon as this wretched war is over that I shall travel, go exploring. Will you come with me?'

Miss Murrell nodded contentedly. She would follow her to the gates of Hell itself if it kept her darling happy.

★ ★ ★

The day passed and Allegra forgot about the two lawyers waiting in the small drawing-room. Her head was full of preparations and plans for the first social gathering to be held at St Osyth's Priory for over four years. She was in her private sitting-room upstairs when

Richard barged in. She frowned.

'You stink of the stable, Richard. Please do not come to me without changing your attire.'

'Stow it, Allegra! We have lawyers to speak to. I gather they have been here all day. If we do not see them now, we shall be obliged to offer them a bed for the night and invite them to dine with us also.'

'God forfend! Did you expect them to come today, Richard?'

'No, but I am eager to hear what they have to say. I have pockets to let and could do with a deal more blunt.'

'Shall I ring and have them shown up?'

Richard shook his head. 'No, I would prefer to speak to them downstairs. Your parlour is not the place for such a meeting.'

They crossed the long, draughty, blue corridor, which even with the substantial fire that was left burning all day remained unpleasantly cool. Allegra shivered and drew her wrap closer, glad she had decided to wear her heavy silk evening gown for the party.

A footman flung open the door to the small drawing-room. Yardley announced them with suitable formality.

'The Right Honourable, the Earl of Witherton and Lady Allegra Humphry.'

The two, tall and slender, as alike as only twins can be, stepped in, prepared to be gracious in spite of the inconvenience of the visit. Richard bowed to the smaller, more rotund of the two gentlemen. He recognized him as Mr Evans, the family lawyer. Who the other hatchet-faced individual was, he had no notion.

'We most sincerely beg your pardon for the unconscionable time you have been kept waiting, sirs. If you had given us due warning of your visit I would, naturally, have been here to greet you this morning.'

Mr Evans returned the bow. 'We have been well looked after, I thank you, my lord. Now we can begin. Lady Allegra, if you would like to be seated?'

She would not, but with compressed lips sailed across the handsome blue French carpet and settled gracefully into a walnut armchair. Richard propped himself against the window and folded his arms. They waited expectantly to hear the good news. Mr Evans turned nervously to his companion.

'This is Mr Southey, he is — '

'Thank you, Evans. I shall take it from here,' the man interrupted rudely. He glared, first at Richard, then at Allegra. She swallowed. This was not as it should be. Why did this obnoxious man need to speak with them?

'I will be candid: it is the only way I deal.

14

Your father gambled your heritage away. He did not kill himself for love, but because he was at *point non plus*. The present owner of the Priory, has, out of the goodness of his heart, allowed you to remain in ignorance of these unpalatable facts, to continue spending his money as if it was water, until he reckoned you were recovered from your grief.' He stared at the ashen-faced couple, satisfied his brutal words were having the desired effect.

'As you are holding a party tonight you have obviously moved on, and are no longer in mourning, and are ready to face up to things.'

Allegra recovered the power of speech. 'But our settlements? The money from our mother's estate, surely we still have that?'

The monster shook his head. 'Nothing left. All gone. My employer holds the deeds to the estate, all of it. You are destitute. You have been living on another man's charity long enough. It is time you learnt the harsh realities of life; discovered what it is like to be hungry, to have to work for your living like ordinary folks do.'

Finally Richard found his voice. It was reed thin. 'How long do we have?'

'Until the end of the month. Then you will vacate these premises.' His lips curled. 'And do not think that you can carry away the furniture and fittings. All you can take are your clothes and your jewellery.' He snorted angrily. 'You would not even have that, if I had my way.' He nodded to Mr Evans, whose eyes glittered damply in the candlelight. 'I shall wait outside for you, Evans. You will not be long.'

2

Mr Evans wrung his hands. 'This is a black day. A black day indeed. Have you much jewellery, Lady Allegra?'

'Nothing that I can sell. They are all priceless heirlooms that have been in the family for hundreds of years.'

'For God's sake, Allegra. It is too late for such niceties. You heard the man, we are all but penniless. This is not the time for scruples.'

'How can you say so? Remember who we are, Richard.'

'Who are we? We will be nothing without the Priory. We have to have funds in order to find somewhere to live, to pay our bills.'

Allegra felt hysteria bubbling up inside her. She needed to escape from this nightmare. How could Richard dismiss it so calmly — their lives were over, couldn't he see that? Stiffly, she pushed herself upright, her movements that of an old woman. 'I am going to my room. I cannot deal with this now.'

She stumbled upstairs, her remaining strength focused on reaching the privacy of her chamber and swallowing sufficient laudanum to

17

send her into the sweet darkness she desperately needed. Her dresser, Abbott, took one look at her face and sent a chambermaid running for Miss Murrell.

Downstairs, Richard turned away and leant his face against the coolness of the leaded window, trying to make sense of what had happened. Half an hour ago he had been rich, master of all he surveyed, now he was just another impecunious aristocrat.

He groaned. 'Mr Evans, who owns St Osyth Priory now?'

'A businessman from Cornwall, Mr Silas Tremayne. He has tin mines, manufactories and ships; he is as rich as Croesus.'

Richard was impressed. 'He could have thrown us out after the funeral. We must, I suppose, be grateful he allowed us the extra nine months.'

'Indeed you must, my lord. I do not know of any other man who would have done the same. Have you any idea how much you and Lady Allegra have spent since last July?'

Richard shook his head. Such matters had never concerned either of them. There had always been ample to sustain their extravagant lifestyle. The estate included several villages as well as gravel pits, a brick yard, timber and dozens of well-run farms to support it.

Mr Evans named a sum that made even Richard blush. 'Good God! That much? I had no idea keeping an establishment in Town was so costly. This man, Tremayne, he owns the London house, and the other estates in Suffolk and Kent as well?'

Mr Evans nodded. 'All of it, your lordship.'

The clock chimed five times and Richard swore. 'God's teeth! Our guests will be arriving in an hour. I have yet to put them off.' He yanked the bell strap and nodded dismissal to the lawyer. 'Can you come back tomorrow, Mr Evans, and go through things when I have had time to adjust?'

'Yes, my lord. This has been a black day, a very black day.'

'So you have said. I bid you good day. Show Mr Evans out, and send Yardley to me at once.' The footman, who had answered the summons, bowed the lawyer from the room.

Richard paced, waiting for the butler to arrive. 'Yardley, I wish you to send messages to both Great Bentley and Frating Hall. Inform them that the dinner tonight is cancelled. Also let the kitchens know.'

Yardley bowed, his lined face impassive. 'Yes, my lord. I'll see to it at once. Will there be anything else?'

Richard barely restrained himself from screaming his answer. 'No, Yardley, thank you.'

He needed to get out of the house, clear his head, or better, drown his sorrows. He did not wish to be alone. He would unearth Gideon and together they could ride across to Weeley. There were always officers at the barracks ready to share a bottle, or three, of claret.

★ ★ ★

Miss Murrell forgot decorum and ran along the draughty corridor. Jenny had said the matter was extremely urgent.

'Abbott, what is wrong?'

'Oh, madam, I am glad you're here. Her ladyship is that distraught, she is searching for the laudanum. The state she is in I fear to give it to her, but if I don't, I'm certain she will dismiss me.'

'Leave it to me, Abbott.' Miss Murrell held out her hand and closed her fingers around the small, deep blue, ridged bottle. 'I will ring if I need you again.'

She could hear the crashes and thuds of articles being thrown and her heart sank even lower. It was years since Allegra had resorted to hurling objects to vent her spleen. With some trepidation she pushed the bedchamber door open.

'Miss Murrell, I insist you give me the

20

laudanum. I shall not be denied.' Allegra's smooth chignon was in disarray and her pale cheeks had a hectic flush. She saw that her companion was secreting what she wanted. 'I demand that you give it to me. Now. At once.'

Her imperious hand was ignored. Miss Murrell gestured towards the old-fashioned Dutch bedstead, its moulded panels and carved lion masks enough to give the most sanguine of sleepers nightmares. It was small wonder Allegra slept poorly.

'Hush, my dear. You shall have it in a moment. First, let me assist you to disrobe. You do not wish to sleep in your gown, surely?'

Allegra stared in confusion; first at her gown then at her companion. Slowly she regained control. 'Papa killed himself because he had gambled away the estate. Richard and I have nothing; we are destitute. We have been ordered to vacate the Priory by the end of the month.'

'Good heavens, child, that is scarcely two weeks away. Where shall we go at such short notice?'

Dry-eyed Allegra collapsed on to the bed. 'I do not know. Richard insists I must sell my jewellery to fund the removal. How can I part with Mama's heirlooms so easily? Does he not understand they are all I have left to remember her by?'

'Put your faith in the Lord, my dear. That is the best thing. Pray hard for an answer and He will give you what you ask. It might not be what you want, but He will answer your prayers, I promise.'

'I will try. I wish I had your certainty, but after what has happened these past two years I find myself unable to trust, as I once did.'

Miss Murrell completed her task and assisted Allegra into bed. Then she carefully removed the stopper from the bottle and tipped a generous measure on to the silver spoon kept ready by the bed.

'Here, my dear. I do not approve of your use of this, but tonight I consider is one of those exceptional occasions when it is allowed.'

Gratefully the girl swallowed the syrup and lay back on the pillows. Miss Murrell pulled up a small tapestry chair and sat down beside the bed.

'I shall stay with you until you fall asleep, my dear. Now, close your eyes, let the laudanum do its work. Tomorrow is soon enough to worry about the future.'

As her eyelids fluttered down Allegra remembered it was her name day. The day she and Richard had been expecting to host their very first dinner together. Instead they had discovered that for the past nine months they had been living on charity and that the father they had always honoured and respected, had feet of clay.

She didn't hear Richard and Gideon gallop off into the twilight. She was in a deep, dreamless sleep.

The Red Lion, Colchester

Silas Tremayne prowled back and forth in his private parlour, stopping every few minutes to stare out of the window and down into the yard. Damn the man, where was he? He had carefully chosen Southey to deliver his message, not Evans, because he wished his victims to be suitably crushed by his news.

His breath hissed through his clenched teeth. There, it was the carriage at last. Unable to remain in his rooms he pounded down the stairs and met Evans and Southey as they entered the inn.

'Well, is it done?'

'It is, sir, exactly as you requested.' Southey smiled as he recalled the shocked expressions when he had delivered the ultimatum. 'Hardly a peep out of either of them. I promise they will not kick up a dust; they will leave like lambs on the appointed date.'

Tremayne's expression hardened. 'Your job is done, Mr Southey. Take your money and make yourself scarce.' He tossed a bulging purse at the man, who caught it deftly.

'You know where to find me, sir, if you should have need of my services again.'

Silas Tremayne turned to the lawyer his expression almost friendly. 'Come up, Mr Evans, and tell me exactly what happened. I wish to know every detail, however insignificant.'

Over two bottles of port the story unfolded. He was not displeased by what he heard. 'So, they are expecting to be evicted in less than two weeks?' Mr Evans nodded. 'Don't look so downcast, man, it will not come to that. I could not tell you the whole before, you had to believe what Southey told them.'

'Believe? Is it not true then, sir? Will Lady Allegra and Lord Witherton be able to stay on at the Priory?'

Tremayne smiled slightly and poured himself another brimming glass. 'As you know I have more money than I could spend in ten lifetimes. Good God, I could buy and sell half the aristocrats in London and still see change.' He swallowed deeply and wiped his mouth on his cuff. 'But, do you know, Evans, I am still *persona non grata* at the best homes. I belong to all the right clubs, dress at

Weston's, and own a townhouse in the fashionable part of London, but the tabbies won't have me. I am a *cit*! They would rather welcome an impoverished *émigré* than invite me into their houses.'

He paused as he considered the injustice of it all. Leaning forward, he stared blearily at his companion. 'Why is that, Evans? Why is that?'

Not sure if the question was rhetorical Evans hesitated. But seeing Mr Tremayne was expecting an answer he told him what he already knew. 'You do not have the pedigree, sir. Money counts, but in some circles bloodlines are everything.'

Tremayne banged the table, sending both glasses flying. 'Exactly! So I decided if I could not buy my way into society I would marry into it. My daughter Demelza will marry the earl and my grandchildren will be aristocrats. How is that for a man descended from Cornish tin miners?'

Mr Evans righted the glasses and refilled them. 'I should have guessed, sir. A real villain would never have allowed Lady Allegra and Lord Witherton to remain so long or paid all their living expenses.'

'He will agree, won't he, Evans? My girl is pretty and she has little to say for herself. That would be considered an advantage by many men, wouldn't it?'

The lawyer drained his glass feeling happier than he had for months. 'He will bite your hand off in his eagerness. But forgive me, sir, I must warn you his lordship is a pleasant enough young man but not what I would call *good husband* material. He gambles and drinks to excess and runs a string of expensive ladybirds.'

Tremayne yawned. 'But he will not continue in that vein, I promise you. I shall keep a tight hold on the purse strings. I might be rich, but I'm not stupid.' He pushed himself upright, swaying a little. 'Good God, I'm foxed! I had no idea I had consumed so much. I'm going to my bed, Mr Evans. I will bid you goodnight.'

'What time will you be visiting the Priory tomorrow, sir?'

'Not before noon. Come to me here at eleven o'clock, there are some documents I have had drawn up, and I would like a second opinion.'

Mr Evans bowed, almost losing his balance. 'I should be honoured, sir. Good-night until the morning.'

Silas Tremayne walked unsteadily to the door that led to his bedchamber and, neglecting to lower his head swore viciously as he reeled back. 'God dammit, Sam

Perkins, why didn't you warn me to duck?'

His valet, and friend, grinned unsympathetically. 'I would have, sir, if I'd known you was coming in at that precise moment.'

'I need a — '

'It's in that closet, sir. Mind your head!' Years of living with his formidable master had inured him to his moods. He knew, as probably no other did, that under the brusque exterior lurked a much gentler man.

★ ★ ★

Breakfast was taken in the private parlour. 'I have a damnable headache, Sam. Have you any of your quackery to fix it?' He flinched as he turned his head too quickly.

'I do, sir. It is by your plate. It don't taste too clever but it will do the trick.'

Tremayne peered suspiciously into the pewter pot. 'If it tastes as vile as it smells, Sam, I might well cast up my accounts.'

'Drink it down in one. It will clear your head and settle your digestion, sir.'

He did as instructed and the bitter liquid, for a moment, threatened to return. Then, miraculously, his head stopped thumping and he could view the assembled dishes with more favour.

'Are the trunks packed, Sam? We will be

leaving here this morning. Our residence from today will be at St Osyth's Priory.' He drained his tankard of porter before continuing. 'Demelza will be arriving later, keep an eye on her for me, I'm going to look at the castle. It's Norman you know.'

'Maybe Miss Demelza would like to see the castle with you, sir; I know she likes historical things.'

'Does she?' He shrugged. 'How do you know that? She never mumbles more than yes or no to me.'

'You're still a stranger to her, sir. Remember you sent her away to school when Mrs Tremayne died and she was but seven years old. And how often have you seen her in the past few years?'

Silas frowned. 'There was no place in my life for a child. I was abroad or busy on business. I saw her when I could.'

'As I said, sir, she's barely acquainted with you. She's still shy. She will come round when she knows you better.'

'Come round? Confound it, Sam, she's my daughter. My own flesh and blood, why is she shy with me?'

That Sam could answer. 'Have you looked at yourself in the glass lately, sir?'

'In the glass? What the devil are you talking about? Why should I do that? I leave my appearance to you.'

Sam grinned. 'There is a glass over the mantel; take a look: you might be surprised.'

He strode over to stand glaring into the mirror. What game was Sam playing with him? Then, as he looked, his expression changed. He began to see what Sam was getting at. The tall dark man staring back at him was almost a stranger. Somewhere, over the years, the slim, casually dressed Cornishman he had been, had metamorphosed into a broad-shouldered, immaculately dressed, worldly gentleman. From the top of his elegantly cropped black hair down to his shiny top boots he was perfectly turned out. His dark-blue, square-fronted coat, his crisply starched cravat with its single diamond pin, his pale-blue waistcoat and calfskin inexpressibles screamed wealth and quality.

'I've turned into a veritable tulip, have I not, Sam? Small wonder my Demelza does not recognize me. Ten years has seen changes in us both. I left a little girl; she has returned from her seminary a young woman.'

Sam busied himself stacking the dirty crockery on the trays. 'Does Miss Demelza know she is to be married?'

'No, of course not. Why should she? Surely it is every debutante's dream to marry an earl? She will be delighted. What girl would

29

not be? I would not have selected young Witherton if he had not been personable. I'm not completely heartless, Sam.'

Sam held his peace. He had said more than enough for one morning and even his privileged position could become precarious if he continued to criticize his employer.

St Osyth's Priory

The splash of water being poured into a bowl woke Allegra. 'What time is it, Jenny?'

'A little after ten o'clock, my lady.'

'Send Abbot in to me.' She closed her eyes again until she heard the dressing-room door softly open. 'Abbot, put out a riding habit. I shall go out for an hour or two. It will clear my head.'

'Are you still wearing black, my lady? Or shall I put out the green or the blue?'

'Anything, it does not matter. Is Lord Witherton down yet, do you know?'

Her abigail sniffed. 'I don't believe he returned last night, my lady.'

'I suppose Captain Pledger went with him?'

'Yes, my lady.'

Allegra knew if this was the case, her brother would have got quite disgustingly inebriated and gambled away even more money that he did not have. She gasped as an appalling thought struck her. The man who owned her home had been obliged to pay Richard's gambling debts for the past nine months. How dreadful! It was bad enough throwing away one's own money, but to do the same with another's did not bear thinking about.

She threw back the richly embroidered comforter and jumped out of bed. She swayed and steadied herself against the bedpost. Ignoring the proffered hand she straightened and stepped away. She sluiced her face with the tepid water in the bowl and it helped, a little, to banish her dizziness.

Abbot and Jenny deftly dressed her in a plain, dove-grey morning gown. The close-fitting three-quarter sleeves and scooped neckline emphasized her thinness and lack of womanly curves. It was not a frock she would have selected for herself, but that morning she was too preoccupied to notice her apparel.

It was only as she descended the stairs she recalled requesting that Abbot fetch a riding habit. She paused, frowning down at the grey silk. Had she changed her mind? She wished her head was clearer. Although she craved the oblivion the syrup gave her, she hated the way it clouded her intellect, making it difficult to think.

She hesitated, debating whether she should go back and change. Did she really wish to ride? She shook her head, the gesture almost causing her to fall. No, it would be foolish to ride out as she was. It would be best to wait until the afternoon. She usually felt fully restored by then. She continued down, trying to remember what it was she wished to discuss with Richard, but it eluded her. Perhaps after she had broken her fast it would come back.

Yardley, waiting in the vast, cold entrance hall, bowed and silently held out a salver upon which was a letter sealed with a blob of red wax. Allegra took it, not recognizing the bold black scrawl on the front. Surprised the missive was addressed to her, not her brother, she took it straight to the window to open. There were no flowery greetings, no commonplace remarks.

It stated simply:

Lady Allegra Humphry
I shall be arriving at noon today. I shall
require two apartments prepared.
Respectfully yours,
Silas Tremayne Esq.

Her eyes blurred and she blinked furiously, such weakness should never be revealed in front of one's staff.

'Have Mrs Wright attend me immediately. I shall be in the small drawing-room.' The butler turned to go but she called him back. 'Yardley, has Lord Witherton returned?'

'Yes, my lady, he is in the breakfast parlour with the captain.'

The thought of food nauseated her, but if she wished to speak to her brother she would have to join him. She sincerely hoped his head was clearer than hers. It seemed that they were not to be allowed even the promised two weeks' grace to put their shattered lives in order, for in less than two hours the new owner of their beloved home was coming to take up residence.

3

Lord Witherton's jaw dropped. 'Good God! Gideon, are you beef witted?'

Captain Pledger's eyes darkened and his fists clenched under the table cloth. 'Why not, Richard? My pedigree is impeccable and that is of more importance to Lady Allegra than whether I am purse pinched, surely?'

'Well, I wish you luck, but do not be surprised if you receive a scaly reception.' The rattle of crockery alerted Richard to the fact that they were no longer private. 'Is Lady Allegra down yet?'

The young footman bowed. 'I'll go and enquire, my lord.' He returned with the news that she was with the housekeeper.

'I have a damnable headache, Gideon. I had far too much brandy last night and far too little sleep. I shall stretch out in the study for an hour or so; maybe I shall feel more the thing later.'

Gideon watched his friend stroll, yawning and rubbing his eyes, from the breakfast parlour. Everything seemed so easy for him; even the possibility of penury and eviction slipped over him leaving him unscathed. Lord

Witherton appeared to believe that a solution to this problem would be presented to them on a silver platter. It always had, so why should it be any different now?

He scowled at the injustices of life. He had deliberately befriended Richard when he had first arrived at school. It had been a lucrative move; over the years his *friend* had supplied him with funds that had been more than enough to allow him to live above the modest income of a serving captain in the Royal Horse Artillery.

Now his finances would be in ruins. This month's gambling debts and mess bill were already double his expected income. His lips curled in a thin smile. If he could persuade Lady Allegra to marry him, he would get his hands on the Witherton jewels. He had seen Lady Allegra wearing a sapphire and diamond parure at her come-out ball several years ago and he had heard an onlooker state it to be worth a king's ransom.

The sale of just those jewels alone would set him up nicely, but first he had to convince the lady herself that his offer was the solution to her problems. He pushed his chair back and surveyed his reflection, fragmented in the window panes. He had dressed with care. His navy regimental jacket was spotless, the gold braid that ran from shoulder to waist shining brightly. His blue trousers, with their bright red seam, were carefully pressed and they hung, as they should, over his black polished boots. He had only to arrange his pelisse, with its black fur lining, over his left shoulder and he would be ready. What woman would be able to resist him in his finest regimentals?

Before pulling on his gloves he smoothed back his dark hair and straightened his stock. The black-and-white plumes on his shako danced as he snatched it from the table and tucked it under his arm. He paused, should he return to his apartment for his sword? No, that would be doing it too brown.

He emerged into the passageway, his boots loud on the polished boards. As he hesitated, a footman hurried up to him, as all the indoor staff, eager to help.

'Is Lady Allegra free?' Captain Pledger asked.

'Yes, sir, Mrs Wright has returned to her duties.'

The captain nodded curtly and, back ramrod stiff, marched along the endless chilly corridor to halt outside the small drawing-room door, waiting for the footman to slide in front of him and open it.

★　★　★

Allegra had not enjoyed her brief meeting with the housekeeper. To be obliged to tell one's staff that from that very afternoon they would be answerable to another, would no longer apply to her for their instructions, was not a pleasant task, but it had had to be done. Richard, as always, would let inertia be his master.

She shuddered at the image of a veritable mushroom and his family occupying St Osyth's Priory. Hundreds of years of Witherton blood had graced these halls; how could she bear to think of what was coming next? Her ancestors would be dancing in their graves with rage.

She looked round, as a footman appeared at the door. 'The Honourable Gideon Pledger, Captain of the Royal Horse Artillery, to see you, my lady.'

She was struck dumb at the sight of such unexpected magnificence so early in the day. Then she guessed his intentions. He had been recalled to duty and had come to make his adieus. A trifle overdressed, perhaps, but the thought of his coming departure softened her normal hauteur.

Emboldened by what he took to be her approval Gideon flung his shako on a convenient settle and dropped dramatically to one knee, grabbing her pale hands as he did so. She froze with horror and attempted to extract them from his vice-like grip, to stop him before he made a complete cake of himself.

So lost in his determination to speak his piece Gideon, normally the first to spot a slight, failed to detect her repulsion, to note the rigidity of her pose.

'Captain Pledger, please stand up. You have quite mistaken the matter. This will not do.'

He ignored her, in his arrogance believing they were but maidenly protestations only to be expected in such circumstances.

'My dearest Lady Allegra. I have always held you in the highest esteem but had, until now, considered you above my touch. I am offering you the protection of my name, my heart, and everything that I own. Would you do me the inestimable honour of becoming my wife?' His grey eyes blazed with sincerity; he knew he had never looked finer. 'Please, make me the happiest of men.'

Allegra stared down, revolted by this unnecessary and embarrassing display. What was the wretched man thinking of? She had made her dislike of him quite plain these past months.

'Release me, sir, this instant! How dare you presume to touch me and refer to me in such familiar terms?' His gloves opened and she snatched back her crushed fingers and backed away rapidly, putting the width of the room between them, before she ventured to speak again. 'Get up from the floor. You are making an exhibition of yourself.' She watched, as the man, his face a mask of hate, sprang to his feet.

'You think you are too good for me? You have always held too high an opinion of yourself. I offered out of pity, nothing else. What normal man would wish to be shackled to a cold, skinny beanpole like you?'

Shocked by his venom she was unable to answer, to offer him even a crumb of comfort to save his pride. Instead she spoke without thought, turning a disappointed man into an implacable enemy.

'I would sooner marry in the stable than ally myself to a man such as you. You are a parasite. My brother has an open nature and he has never understood that your friendship was purely mercenary. But, like a rat in a sinking ship, you will desert him now.' She lifted her head. 'Your immediate departure is the one ray of sunshine in all this misery. I do not wish to see you here again, Captain Pledger; do I make myself clear?'

For a moment she saw his right shoulder bunch, as if he was thinking of striking her, but he picked up his hat and bowed formally, his temper under control, the epitome of politeness.

'I shall bid you good day, my lady.' She nodded and raised her head. His eyes bored into hers. 'You will live to regret this; you will discover that even the mighty can fall and they have the furthest to go.'

The door slammed behind him rattling the glassware in a tall walnut cabinet. Allegra remained staring at the door for almost a minute, her feet refusing to obey her command. Her knees felt weak and she knew she had to sit down before she collapsed.

Somehow she groped her way to the padded settle. Her hands were shaking too much to reach out for the bell. She had never liked Pledger, but only now, when it was too late, did she realize he was not the weak man she had always thought him.

Slowly she regained control and reached for the bell. Richard had still to be told that the new owners, the unspeakable encroachers, the Tremaynes, would arrive in less than one and a half hours. Richard, who had been dozing in the library, was not pleased to be summoned to his sister's side.

'What is it, Allegra, can a man not have a bit of shut-eye in peace any more?'

Allegra hesitated. Should she tell him about Pledger or Tremayne first? 'Captain

Pledger has left, Richard.'

'I am not surprised. Gave him his *congé* did you? I told him not to approach you, but he would do it.'

'Well, you could have warned me, and thus avoided an uncomfortable ten minutes for both of us.'

'Is that all, my dear? If so, I will toddle along and — '

'No, Richard it is not all. Mr Tremayne and his family are arriving here in one hour and thirty minutes.'

'The devil take it! Whatever for?'

'To take up residence, you nincompoop, why else?'

He shook his head and instantly regretted it. 'I have not sorted out my belongings, nor arranged our lodgings; how can we be expected to leave at such short notice?'

'We do not have to leave. We have two weeks, remember? But the man owns the property; he is entitled to live here. Why should he wait until we have gone? The place is large enough to lose an army in, for heaven's sake.'

'Where have you put them?'

'In the west wing. He has asked for two apartments to be prepared so he must be bringing his family with him. Do you know if he is married?'

'I have no idea.' He sighed loudly and scratched his poorly shaven jaw. 'I suppose I had better change into my finest. Thunder and turf — do the staff know?'

'Yes, Richard. I informed Mrs White earlier and I have asked her to speak to Yardley; he will do the rest.'

'This is a bad day, my dear. But we shall come about, never fear.'

'Miss Murrell suggested that I put my faith in the Lord, are you of the same mind, Richard?'

He grinned. 'Fate, faith, call it what you will, something always comes up. Shall we go up? I am certain that you do not wish to meet the new owners dressed in that gown.'

'Indeed I do not. I do not know, quite, how it is I am wearing such a monstrosity, but I intend to find out.'

★　★　★

Word had spread around the staff long before Allegra reached her apartments. Her dresser and maid were waiting for her. 'Abbott, I have come to change this hideous frock. And by the way, why am I wearing it, I thought I had asked for my riding habit?'

Abbot dropped a curtsy. 'You were not well enough to ride, and this was the first gown I could lay my hands on. I apologize, my lady, if I overstepped myself.'

Allegra smiled. 'No, you were quite right, but please dispose of this object. I am sure a member of the deserving poor would appreciate it more than I.'

'I have got out a selection of gowns, my lady; I thought you might like to select the ensemble yourself.'

An array of colour greeted her arrival in her bedchamber. No lavenders, nor greys, and definitely no black. She was about to protest but, for once, thought for a moment.

'Yes, Abbott, you are right. I shall wear colour. Are these the gowns we ordered last month?'

'They are, my lady. The amber silk, with the pale-gold bodice is a lovely gown. See the pretty corded tassels in gold braid that tie the sleeve points, they exactly match the bugle beads around the hem.'

'Yes. I will wear that one. And I think I will wear a corset. Do not look so astounded, it is *de rigueur*, surely?'

'But, your ladyship, pardon me for saying so, but you have no need for such restraint.'

'I know, but at least it will push what little bosom I have upwards and give me a more feminine outline.'

Her dresser and maid exchanged looks but

did as they were bid.

The gown was a trifle loose but the high waist concealed this discrepancy well. Abbott fastened the clasp of the double row of amber beads and stepped back, satisfied she had done her job well.

'There, your ladyship, you look like a princess.'

Allegra frowned. 'I think the gold ribbons threaded through my hair are a mistake, but it is too late to remove them.'

'Oh no, Lady Allegra, they add the finishing touch. Your chignon is the same, none of the ringlets or trailing bits you so dislike.'

'It will do, thank you, Abbott. Did you take the message to Miss Murrell earlier, Jenny?'

'Yes, my lady. Miss Murrell said as she would check the apartments before she comes to you in your parlour. I believe I heard a tap on the door, it will be Miss Murrell now.'

Allegra heard her companion chatting to Jenny and swept from the bedchamber to join her.

'Lady Allegra! How lovely you look, my dear. I had quite forgotten how beautiful you are. Black is not a flattering colour, especially for someone as fair as you.'

'Thank you, Miss Murrell. And your gown

is perfect. Dark green is such a practical colour, is it not?'

Abbott appeared and draped a gossamer thin, gold cashmere wrap around her shoulders.

'The blue corridor is cold and you could be waiting there a while; you do not wish to catch a chill, my lady.'

'No, thank you, Abbott. Come, Miss Murrell, shall we go down? The Tremaynes are due to arrive at any minute.'

Allegra held her shawl close, knowing that short sleeves, however attractive, were not a good choice for April. Although the building they resided in was mainly modern, having been constructed by their grandfather, it was so vast it was impossible to keep it at a pleasant temperature. Richard was resplendent in bottle-green superfine and cream inexpressibles, his pale gold waistcoat a perfect foil for his sister's gown. He scanned her appearance and nodded, pleased she had on something attractive.

'Come and stand by the fire. Yardley has instructions to assemble the staff as soon as the carriage turns into the park.'

'Has their baggage arrived?'

Yes, about an hour ago. They should be content in the west wing; at least they will be warmer over there.'

'Have they brought many staff?'

'A couple of maids and a valet came in the carriage; they are unpacking. I have had Yardley clear out Gideon's apartment. Half his belongings were left behind. I have had them parcelled up and I shall take them up to Town when I go next.'

Allegra forced her mouth to curve. 'I should not bother. He will have attached himself to someone else by then and those garments will have been replaced.'

'I hope you let him down kindly, Allegra. He has long held a *tendre* for you.'

She swallowed. 'Any refusal is a dent for a man's pride, Richard, but I am sure he will recover soon enough.'

From her station by the window Miss Murrell exclaimed, 'Oh my, I can see the carriage. It is drawn by three pairs of black horses, what a splendid equipage.'

Richard tugged the bell; the signal for Yardley to assemble all the indoor staff who could be spared from their duties, and for the heavy front door to be opened. He took Allegra's arm and was surprised to discover it trembling.

'This will not be so bad, Allegra; the man cannot be a monster. After all, he has allowed us nine months' grace at his expense.'

'He is a usurper, a man of no breeding, and

46

he now has your birthright. How can you be so sanguine?'

They positioned themselves carefully, so they could observe but remain hidden in the darkness of the house. The carriage drew up in a scrunch of gravel and dust. Six grooms leapt forward whilst footmen opened the door and let down the steps.

A tall, very tall man with chiselled features, weather-beaten complexion and cropped black hair, emerged first. He was, Richard noticed, dressed to perfection, no expense spared, every item proclaiming him a top of the trees sort of gentleman. He smiled, beginning to relax, believing that just possibly the Priory might be in safe hands.

Allegra's teeth clenched as he turned to assist a much younger woman, in fact no more than a girl, from the carriage. This young woman was like a drab country mouse compared to the magnificence beside her. Her bonnet was plain straw with a single dark-blue ribbon, her pelisse dark, of indeterminate colour, and quite definitely years behind fashion.

How could Mr Tremayne dress himself so well and have his daughter, for she was far too young to be his spouse, dress like a governess? He was a millionaire! Why would he allow a member of his family to walk around like this? Had the man no idea how to behave? Did he understand what was expected from an owner of the Priory?

Rigid with indignation she waited beside her brother for the Tremaynes to come in to take possession of their new home. She already held the impeccably dressed gentleman in dislike; his callous treatment of his daughter merely reinforced her disapproval.

Yardley bowed deeply and led the party inside.

4

'Where are we going to live, Papa? Tell me again, please,' Demelza asked, eyes shining with excitement.

'We are going to live at a place called St Osyth Priory, a magnificent building that, in parts, harks back to the thirteenth century or even earlier.'

'Please do not misunderstand me, you know that I love the house you have built for us at Pencarrow, it has every modern convenience and is neither too large nor too small, but it is not old.'

Tremayne chuckled. 'No, my love, that is quite true, but then neither is the main part of the Priory.'

'Oh, do not laugh at me. You know what I mean.' She giggled, feeling more relaxed in his company than since she had joined him in London, three weeks previously. 'Is it far from Colchester, this Priory?'

'No, we should be here soon. Watch the scenery, Demelza, it is very — '

'Scenic?' she enquired, still laughing.

Tremayne's eyes narrowed and he stared at his daughter. Had he been mistaken? Her heart-shaped face and thick black ringlets, dominated by eyes of a hue close to violet, was the image of her dead mother but the intelligence and humour she was demonstrating could not have come from her. He grinned, his face at once appearing younger and less forbidding.

'Baggage! I can see the demure face you have been showing me is but a façade. You're more like me than I realized.'

She nodded, happy that his comment was a compliment. 'At school I was expected to set a good example to the younger girls, but now I am released I can express my opinions more freely.'

He had a moment's misgiving. He had learnt more about his daughter in the short journey than he had in the past few weeks. He hoped Sam Perkins was not right; that Demelza would not cavil at his plan to marry her to Lord Witherton.

The coach, manufactured especially for him in London, was as comfortable as any vehicle could be on the rutted country lanes. Two grooms travelled on the step at the rear, all armed and prepared to defend their employer and his daughter to the death from any footpads or highwayman lurking hopefully in empty stretches of heath land or roadside coppice.

A little after one o'clock the carriage bowled up a gentle slope in the lane and turned in through an impressive gate. The gatekeeper and his wife bowing and smiling as they rumbled past.

Tremayne sat forward. 'We shall soon be there, Demelza. This drive takes us through the park — you will see the lake on your right.'

'May I lower the window, Papa, so that I can lean out?'

'Certainly not; we shall be visible in a mile or so and I do not wish you to be seen at the window like an urchin when we arrive.'

She had to content herself with gazing out of the window, catching tantalizing glimpses of the extensive grounds in between the branches of the avenue of trees they were travelling down. The carriage slowed as it reached the turning circle in front of the north side of the Priory.

Tremayne waited for his daughter's reaction. He was not disappointed. 'Oh, Papa, look! There is a tower and ruins. It is like something from a fairy tale.'

'It is said to be the finest example of its kind in the country,' he told her proudly.

Tremayne picked up his beaver and put it under his arm. Demelza, more aware than her father that her outfit, perfectly acceptable at her exclusive seminary, made her look like his poor relation, straightened her bonnet, which had slipped somewhat askew over the twelve-mile journey.

The carriage was halted adjacent to an ancient edifice which immediately caught her attention and she forgot her sartorial shortcomings completely. Tremayne waited, as was expected, until the footmen had lowered the steps.

He turned to assist his daughter. 'Come alone, my dear, it is time to introduce ourselves.' He pulled her arm through his and they began to stroll towards the open front door. He narrowed his eyes but could see nothing in the darkness of the hall. He knew, of course, what the earl looked like; tall, of slender build, but a young Adonis, guaranteed, he hoped, to make his daughter's heart beat faster.

Lady Allegra he had never seen. She had had her two seasons before he purchased his townhouse and started frequenting the haunts of the *haut ton*. But her beauty was legendary. He knew she had collected and refused a dozen offers from a variety of eligible bachelors. Rumour had it that none of them had come up to her high standards; only a duke would do. Then the countess had been taken grievously ill and Lady Allegra had not appeared in town again.

It was for her sake that he had allowed them to keep the king's ransom in jewellery. He did not wish to see her dowerless. With these as her settlement she could still attract a nobleman whose birth matched her own.

He smiled; if she was as lovely as her reputation, fortune or not, she would find herself a husband soon enough. As soon as Demelza was safely shackled to the earl he would encourage Lady Allegra to find herself a mate. He knew his daughter would never be accepted as the countess if Lady Allegra was still in residence.

He felt the fingers on his arm tighten and he patted them. 'You are anyone's equal, my dear. Remember what I have always told you: it's what's inside a man that counts. A long pedigree does not make you better than your peers; it merely makes you think you are.'

The butler stepped forward and bowed low, then introduced himself and the housekeeper. The black-garbed gentleman ushered them into the blue corridor, past ranks of smartly dressed staff, bowing and curtsying.

'Good grief! This place is cold as a tomb — have you no fires lit?' He sensed disapproval wafting towards him from the matching pair standing in the centre of the room, waiting for him to introduce himself.

He strode forward, his features perfectly controlled, determined to get this difficult five minutes completed, so he could take possession of his property and state his requirements to the young man watching him warily from half-closed, pale-blue eyes. Tremayne bowed to Richard.

'Lord Witherton, Silas Tremayne, at your service.' He turned to the tall, pale girl standing silently beside the earl. 'Your servant, Lady Allegra.' He bowed again and for the first time really saw the young woman. His eyes widened in appreciation.

★ ★ ★

Lady Allegra saw naked desire flare in the eyes of the man who had come to steal away her heritage and knew that the balance of power had changed. She had seen the look many times before. She had found that men were drawn to her coolness; all thought themselves to be the one Prince Charming who could win her for themselves.

They all believed, quite erroneously, that her remoteness held a fiery centre. She knew it did not. She was as she seemed, a lovely, reserved aristocrat. This had been her true reason for refusing all the offers. She could not bear the thought of exposing her most intimate self to another and then for him to find her wanting and turn away in disgust, to return to his mistress for his pleasure. She had watched her mother live a life hidden away in the shadows for that very reason.

The countess had tried to convince Allegra that the arrangement was quite acceptable, that her life was more comfortable that way. But Allegra had known just how much her poor father had loved his undemonstrative wife. A true relationship between a man and his wife should include all aspects, including the marriage bed.

She watched, unmoved, as Tremayne banked down the fire and schooled his features. She nodded, naturally she did not curtsy to him, and waited for him to introduce the girl.

'Lady Allegra, may I introduce my daughter, Miss Demelza Tremayne.'

The girl, as she had been taught, sank into graceful curtsy, keeping her eyes demurely to the floor. She noted the neat figure, disguised under the hideous garments, and decided the young lady could definitely dress to advantage. She could not allow the daughter of the new owner to look like a governess, not when there was something she could do to rectify matters.

Richard bowed, Demelza curtsied and he reached out to take her hand and raise her to her feet. Instead of a whey-faced, solemn schoolgirl he met the eyes of an enchanting Cornish pixie and he smiled down at her.

'I am delighted to meet you, Miss Tremayne. I hope you will be as happy here as we have been.'

'Thank you, my lord. It is such a beautiful place, I'm sure that I shall love it.'

'Allow me to show you around, when you have recovered from your journey, of course.'

Her gurgle of laughter broadened his smile. 'Good heavens, my lord, we have only travelled from Colchester, not Cornwall.'

Allegra decided to intervene. She could not allow Richard to behave in his usual charming, flirtatious manner. Miss Tremayne did not deserve to be treated so casually. 'Miss Tremayne, Mrs Wright is waiting to escort you to your apartments. Please inform her if there is anything that you find lacking.'

Demelza dipped politely. 'Thank you, Lady Allegra. Will I see you before dinner, Papa?'

'It is possible, but I have urgent business to attend to.' He nodded at Richard and Allegra. 'I would like to meet you both, let us say, two hours from now, for there are matters of business we have to discuss.'

As soon as they were alone Allegra felt her

breathing return to normal. 'What an obnoxious mushroom. I cannot wait to leave here. It is unbearable to consider that our ancestral home is now in the possession of that person.'

'My dear, he is not so bad. At least he looks the part, which is more than I can say for his daughter. If she is not careful Miss Tremayne will be mistaken for a maidservant.'

'That is something I intend to take care of, if you will excuse me, Richard. Shall we meet here, later, and go together to hear what is in store for us? No doubt, not content with ruining our father and taking our birthright from us, he now wishes to humiliate us further.'

She didn't wait to hear his reply and swept away, up the plain oak staircase and along the passageway to her apartments. Even with log fires burning in both rooms it was still not warm.

'Abbott,' she called, as she entered. Her dresser instantly appeared. 'Do I still have the trunk of gowns from my comeout season?'

Abbott's brow creased. 'Why, yes, Lady Allegra, I believe they are in a trunk somewhere in the attics.'

'Excellent. Have them sent to Miss Tremayne's apartments. Also I wish to speak to Miss Murrell; Jenny must fetch her.'

Miss Murrell appeared a trifle breathless, believing the summons had sounded urgent. 'How can I be of assistance, my dear? You know I shall help you in any way I can to endure these difficult days.'

'That is as may be. I did not send for you to discuss my problems, but those of Miss Tremayne.'

'Miss Tremayne? I am not sure that I follow, my dear.'

'I would like you to take her in hand, Miss Murrell. As I am now firmly on the shelf, I have no more need of a companion, but Miss Tremayne is seventeen, and would greatly benefit from your advice.'

Miss Murrell's eyes filled. 'Are you dismissing me, Lady Allegra?'

Allegra hurried across and awkwardly hugged the older lady. 'No, no; but you will do better here, my dear Miss Murrell. I will make sure that they double what I have been giving you. You will get to visit Town, attend balls and soirées again, instead of mouldering away in the country with a spinster like me.'

'You are not old enough to live without a companion, my dear. Tongues will wag. Five and twenty does not make you unmarriageable, you know.'

'Let them, I care not. I do not intend to go about in society again. I shall sell some jewellery and buy myself a small house somewhere where I am not known and become an eccentric. Richard shall have the rest and make a new life himself somewhere without me hanging on his coat-tails.' Miss Murrell was about to protest but she forestalled her. 'I have asked for my debutante wardrobe to be sent to Miss Tremayne. She is slightly shorter than I but her figure is similar to mine at that age, and I believe all the gowns will require is taking up at the hem.' She smiled sadly. 'It seems so long ago now. They were lovely, and although styles have changed over the past seven years, dresses are now short-waisted once more and I doubt anyone will notice they are not completely à la mode.'

Miss Murrell smiled. 'The sleeves are more pointed and the hems a little wider but I do believe you are quite correct. Your old gowns will be perfect for Miss Tremayne. It is so obliging of you to think of her at a time like this.'

'Richard says she might be mistaken for a servant as she is. I cannot let that happen when I have dresses to spare. Do you not find it extraordinary that her father is parading like a peacock in his finery whilst his only daughter dresses like a pauper? What sort of parent is he?'

'It is not my place to comment on that, my dear. But he did appear to speak kindly to her. Mrs Wright tells me Miss Tremayne has but recently left a seminary for young ladies in Surrey. Perhaps she is still wearing outfits from that establishment?'

'Very likely. I am sure she will be glad of your expertise with a needle, Miss Murrell. Please devote your time to her in future. I expect I shall see you at dinner. I have arranged for it to be served an hour later, at six; this should give you time enough to help to alter a suitable gown for Miss Tremayne.'

Miss Murrell hurried away and Allegra had forgotten her before the door had quite closed. She needed to think, to find a way to use Tremayne's obvious desire for her to their advantage. Subterfuge was alien to her nature, but when so much was at stake she was prepared to try anything. Perhaps she could fool him into believing she would accept a *carte blanche*; then he would lavish expensive gifts on her, which she could sell and add to her nest egg.

She frowned; what was she thinking of? Such behaviour would make her no better than a light skirt. But could she use her influence to extract promises from him that he would take care of the Priory? That he would honour the family commitment to the long-term well-being of their staff. Staff! What about the dozen or so pensioners living in the whitewashed cottages? Would he continue to take care of old people he had never met and had no connection with him?

She bit her knuckles, trying to still their trembling. She knew what tradespeople were like; she had met Victor Bowers, who had bought up estates locally and turned off half the tenants and squeezed the others almost to bankruptcy.

A gentleman was born; buying up land was not the same as being bred to own it. A gentleman without land was nothing. That was why her father had killed himself. He had been unable to live without his birthright. She scowled. How long did she have before she had to go down for the meeting? Over an hour — time enough to complete the long-walk around the Wilderness and calm her agitation.

★   ★   ★

Tremayne could not remove the image of Lady Allegra from his mind. His nostrils flared and his pulse quickened and he felt an uncomfortable tightness in his groin. She was so fragile, so utterly desirable, her every move a line of poetry. He swung back from his position at the window, angry with himself, and almost snarled at Evans, who was scribbling away like a demented clerk, at the desk.

'How much longer, for God's sake, man? You have been scratching away for almost two hours. How long does it take to write a document?'

Mr Evans replaced his quill in the inkstand and rubbed his aching wrist. 'There, it is done, sir. Exactly as you requested. Now one document states that Lord Witherton must marry Miss Tremayne and the other that Lady Allegra must marry you, if they are to remain in control of the Priory.'

'Good, thank you, Mr Evans. I beg your pardon for speaking so brusquely.'

'No matter. You have weighty matters on your mind.' The lawyer cleared his throat. 'I must point out, Mr Tremayne, as your legal adviser, that I do not approve of the codicil; it is asking for trouble.'

Tremayne grinned. 'It will give them both an illusion of choice. Remember, I did not become a man of substance by being gullible. Whatever scenario they come up with, I shall have the answer, and each time they fail, my grip on the situation will tighten.'

Mr Evans thought it wise not to raise any further objections. 'Have you spoken to Miss Tremayne, sir?'

He shook his head. 'I wish Witherton to offer for her as though it is his own idea. It will make it easier.'

Yardley appeared at the door. 'Yes, sir? You rang?'

'Please convey my compliments to Lord Witherton and Lady Allegra and ask them to join me in the study.'

'Yes, sir. I believe Lord Witherton is outside showing Miss Tremayne the old gatehouse. Her ladyship is walking in the rose garden. I will send someone to fetch them immediately, sir.'

Tremayne turned to Evans. 'Well, Evans, it would appear that my daughter and Witherton are already attracted. All I have to do is give them a nudge.'

★   ★   ★

Richard watched his enchanting new friend run lightly up the stairs, her new afternoon dress, in palest yellow sprigged muslin, floating enticingly out around her brown kid halfboots and white silk stockings. He felt Allegra join him.

'I hardly knew her, what a difference a dress makes.'

'Indeed it does,' she replied drily. 'I was fetched inside. Are we wanted?'

'Yes, Tremayne requests our company in the study. Come along, Allegra, let us get this farce over with.'

But Allegra stood, rooted to the spot. 'I cannot, Richard, please, you know I cannot go into that room.'

5

Richard failed to hear his sister's plea. Allegra watched as he vanished through the door leaving her no choice. She would have to follow him.

She forced her feet to walk towards the one room in the Priory she no longer entered. An attentive footman held open the study door and bowed her through.

'Lady Allegra Humphry.'

Mr Tremayne stood behind the desk, the lawyer, no longer their lawyer it seemed, stood beside him. Richard lounged against the window, his long booted legs crossed at the ankles, his arms folded, apparently at ease. Only Allegra knew how tense he was, what an effort he was making to appear calm. She swallowed hard and clenched her fists. For his sake she would try to be strong, to follow his lead and not reveal her inner turmoil.

'If you will please be seated, Lady Allegra, we can get this over with,' Tremayne said. He indicated a straight-backed chair placed centrally, directly in front of the hated desk. She almost refused; she would much prefer to hide in the shadows by the window with her brother but she had not the strength to argue. Obediently she sat, but unable to look ahead, lowered her eyes and stared at her hands resting on her lap. The dark panelled walls began to press in on her.

Mr Tremayne and Mr Evans took their places. 'Lord Witherton,' Tremayne began, his tone quiet but commanding. 'I have here a document which I shall read to you. Listen carefully; if you agree to the proposals contained therein then you will be required to sign it. Is that clear?'

'Perfectly, Mr Tremayne.'

Allegra heard Mr Tremayne reading but the meaning and content of his words escaped her. She was aware that the voice had stopped.

'Lady Allegra, although this document is directed at Lord Witherton it is essential that you are fully cognizant of its contents as well.'

She raised her head slowly; she had no choice, he was speaking directly to her. It would be unpardonable not to respond. But her eyes did not travel as far as the man watching her closely from his vantage point behind the desk; they froze on the expanse of polished oak in front of him.

She did not see the desk as it was; she saw a pool of blood and the shattered remains of her father's noble face resting in it. Bile rose in her throat and waves of blackness rolled over her.

'Oh please — I cannot . . . do not make me . . . ' Her words were no more than a whisper, then she fell forward from her chair in a swoon.

Tremayne was beside her before Richard had taken more than a step. 'God damn it! I had no wish to distress her so,' Tremayne's voice was loud in the shocked silence. He slid his arms under her body and scooped her up. He glared at Richard, only now reacting. 'Is there a physician locally, Witherton?'

'Yes, in the village.'

'Have him fetched. No, stay here. *I* shall take her to her chamber.' Tremayne glanced over his shoulder at Evans. 'Read the rest to Witherton and have him sign it. I shall be down directly.'

With Allegra unconscious in his arms he followed a footman back to the hall and up the stairs. He was led along another endless freezing passageway. The servant halted before a solid, panelled door and raised his fist to knock.

'Open the door. I wish to get her ladyship into the warm, where she can be attended to by her maidservants.'

He carried his burden, who weighed no

more than a child, into an old-fashioned, but mercifully warm, parlour. Abbott, who had been sitting mending by the window, dropped her sewing in dismay.

'Sir, please bring Lady Allegra straight through to her bedchamber.'

Tremayne did not notice the heavy Dutch furniture, expensive French carpets and massive four-poster bed; his eyes went to the log fire blazing in the grate. 'Thank God! At least it is bearable in here.' He gently placed Allegra on the comforter, stepping back immediately to allow the maids to deal with the patient.

'We were in the study when your mistress swooned.' Abbott's shocked gasp alerted him. 'Was it the room where her father killed himself?'

'Yes, sir. Lady Allegra has not been able to enter it since. She has nightmares still, about it. Seeing her poor father like that; it was not something any gently bred lady should have had to see.'

'I had no idea. But Witherton knew. What was he thinking of? Why didn't he tell me?' He frowned. He would discuss the matter with the young man when he returned to the study. 'Does Lady Allegra have the wasting sickness? She is too thin.'

Abbott shook her head. 'No, sir. But she

has little appetite and sleeps poorly.' She hesitated, considering if it was her place to reveal her mistress's secrets.

He waited for her to continue. He had a shrewd idea what it was she was about to say and why she was reluctant to speak. 'She takes laudanum to help her sleep?'

Relieved he had guessed, Abbott nodded. 'Yes, sir.'

There was a slight noise from the bed. 'I think Lady Allegra's rousing. I'll leave you with her. Has she eaten anything today?'

'I don't believe so.'

'I'll have something sent up to her; see that she eats it. I've also sent for the doctor. I wish her to be examined, just to be sure.'

★ ★ ★

Allegra watched him go. Now she was out of *that* room her head was clear again. For a common person he demonstrated a degree of sensitivity she found surprising. She closed her eyes and tried to recall what he had been saying before she fainted. She shook her head in frustration. She could remember nothing of importance. She would have to wait until Richard came up to see her. He could tell all she needed to know.

'Do you wish to undress, my lady? Remove

that corset so you can breathe properly?'

'I rather think that I do, Abbott. But I shall have to dress for dinner later so my robe will suffice for the present.'

★　★　★

Richard stared at Evans not quite believing what he had heard. 'Let me get this straight, Evans. If I am prepared to marry Miss Tremayne, I have the Priory and all our estates restored to me, debt free, and things will be as before?'

'More or less, my lord. But Mr Tremayne is insistent that Miss Tremayne must be unaware of this arrangement, or there will be no agreement. You have to win her. It must appear to be a love match, or there will be no match at all.'

Richard could hardly believe his luck. He had to marry some time, set up his nursery, and if Miss Tremayne was not exactly what he would have chosen, she was a taking little thing and it would be no hardship to take her to his bed, no hardship at all. He smiled at the lawyer.

'I do not anticipate any difficulty there. Miss Tremayne fancies herself half in love with me already. Hand me the pen, I will sign, and gladly. Marrying beneath me is a small price to pay to regain my heritage.' Neither man had noticed the return of Tremayne.

'How dare you speak of my daughter so disparagingly? Let me tell you, she is worth ten of your kind.'

Richard recoiled at the fury he saw on the other man's face. 'I beg your pardon, sir. No offence intended, I do assure you. I shall be honoured to marry Miss Tremayne. I meant — '

'Don't bother to weasel your way out of it. You do yourself no favours.' He flicked his eyes over Richard and found him wanting. 'I chose you, Witherton, because in spite of your gambling and whoring you do not appear vicious. Also you have the blond looks most young women favour. This matter is not entirely settled. I now have very serious reservations about my decision.'

Richard could feel his lifeline slipping away. He would not be the first, and certainly not the last, impoverished aristocrat to marry an heiress of less than impeccable bloodlines in order to restore his fortunes. He could not let a moment's foolishness ruin his life.

He straightened and took one step closer to the intimidating man who watched him through narrowed eyes. He bowed. 'I appreciate your generosity, sir. I beg your pardon if my thoughtless words offended you. I have been raised to think myself as almost above princes; it has made me overly proud. I can assure you that in future I will be more considerate. I also promise you that I shall treat Miss Tremayne with the utmost respect and consider myself a lucky man indeed if she agrees to be my wife.'

Tremayne considered, his face impassive. He nodded, but his expression remained grim.

'Very well, Witherton, I shall say no more on that subject. However, there is something else I wish to bring to your attention.' Richard ran his finger round his stock which unaccountably seemed overly tight. 'Why did you allow Lady Allegra to come in this room when you know she has not set foot in here since your father killed himself?'

The colour drained from Richard's face and for a moment Tremayne thought he too would swoon. 'Brandy, Evans, quickly.' He pushed Richard roughly on to the chair vacated by his sister earlier and handed him the glass of brandy. 'Here, lad, drink this down in one swallow.'

Immediately Richard drank, the spirit flooded through his veins and slowly his colour returned.

'I had forgotten, sir. How can I have been

so stupid? Oh God! I would never have deliberately caused her such distress — she is my twin — my other half. I would rather die than hurt her.'

To his astonishment Tremayne slapped him on the back and laughed. 'Cut me no Cheltenham tragedies, my boy. Hysterical females are one thing — but young men?'

Richard found himself grinning back. 'I cannot imagine what has come over me today. You must think you are about to tie your daughter to a complete booby.'

'If I thought that, Witherton, I would not be here. Now, do you understand what is required of you?'

'Yes, sir, I do. I am happy to sign. It is more than this family deserves. I shall not let you down.'

'See that you don't. Give him the pen, Evans.' Tremayne watched, a satisfied gleam in his eyes, as the first part of his scheme was finalized. He had chosen well. The boy was ideal for his Demelza. Intelligent, easygoing, and ready to settle down. All that remained was to persuade Lady Allegra to sign her document. Somehow, he thought, that was not going to be as easy to accomplish.

Richard signed his name with a flourish, straightened and nodded. 'If you will excuse me, Mr Tremayne, I wish to go upstairs and apologize to my sister. Has she recovered from her faint?'

'She has. However, I have not cancelled the doctor's visit; it is as well to be sure.' The door closed softly leaving Tremayne and Evans together. 'That went better than I could have anticipated, Evans. Are you sure he understood all the clauses?'

'Does it matter if he did not? He has signed it. He is bound to do as you bid or forfeit his heritage.' Evans sanded the parchment and rolled it carefully before securing it with a silk ribbon. 'Being obliged to give up his mistress and cease gambling is a small price to pay for restoring his home and fortune. He will not object, I am certain of it. He is a decent young man; he has sowed plenty of wild oats and it is time for him to take over the running of the estate and the responsibilities of a wife and family.'

'Leave Lady Allegra's papers with me. I shall speak to her tomorrow morning, when she is fully recovered.'

Evans's brow wrinkled. 'I must warn you, Lady Allegra is not as biddable as Lord Witherton. She has always been the leader, the strong one of the family. She nursed her mother through her illness, gave up her chances of making a brilliant match without a qualm. And she ran the estate, acted for her father and brother, whilst they were gallivanting in Town.'

'I had noticed that the farms and cottages are in excellent repair and the fields in good order. Is that down to her?'

'It is, sir, very keen on looking after her own is Lady Allegra. She believes it is part of her duty to protect and nurture anyone who lives or works on Priory lands.'

Tremayne looked thoughtful. 'Thank you, Evans. I believe that information will prove useful in my quest to win her hand. I shall expect you here by eleven o'clock to complete this business.'

⋆ ⋆ ⋆

Yardley escorted Dr Jones from the Priory and glanced at the tall clock ticking loudly in the corner. Should he remove one set of cutlery from the dining-table, or expect Lady Allegra to come down for dinner? He beckoned over a footman.

'Go upstairs and ask Abbot if her ladyship will be dining downstairs tonight, or if she requires a tray to be sent up later.'

He walked through into the dining-room to inspect the table. The white damask cloth was smooth, the silver candelabra sparkled, ready to be lit. The sconces on the walls, a hangover from a much earlier century, were flickering, throwing golden light onto the heavy polished sideboard.

The massive table was laid for five. Each set of silver cutlery and crystal was isolated by the yards of damask between each setting. He frowned, imagining the difficulty the diners would have conversing if he allowed the table to be left this way. He snapped his fingers.

'Move the settings up to the end of the table. The one nearest the fire.'

The crystal glasses and the bowls of spring flowers were in their new place in minutes. He nodded, satisfied. This dinner was going to be difficult for them; he didn't wish to make it worse.

The footman returned from upstairs. 'Lady Allegra will be coming down, Mr Yardley, sir.'

'Good. Confirm with the kitchen that they will be ready and then ring the gong.'

* * *

Allegra had selected an amber crepe evening gown with an overdress of white sarcenet, trimmed with pearls and having a demi-train. The dress had a light, short jacket, decorated, like the hem, with a single row of pearls.

'At least I do not need a shawl with this costume, Abbot.' She turned sideways to examine her profile. 'The bodice is so well cut that even without a corset I have a semblance of a curve.' She reached up to touch her new hairstyle. For the first time she had allowed it to be dressed in the prevailing fashion, her hair brought together and confined at the back of her head in two light knots, reminiscent of an ancient Roman matron. Then a braid of her pale, white-gold hair had been drawn over a demi-turban, formed from matching amber satin, and the whole finished with rows of pearls and a superb sprig of the same jewels ornamenting the front.

'I hope Mr and Miss Tremayne appreciate the effort you have gone to this evening, Abbot.'

Abbot smiled, certain her mistress had never looked finer. 'If you're ready, Lady Allegra, I believe I heard the gong a few moments ago.'

Richard was waiting in her sitting-room, elegant in black evening dress, his wide shoulders and slim hips shown to advantage by his closely fitting tailcoat and the pantaloons and black slippers he wore. He offered his arm.

'You look wonderfully, my dear. Shall we go down?'

He had not told her the true contents of the document he had signed. When he realized she had not heard anything Tremayne had said he had decided to keep her in ignorance. Instead he had told her that the documents were merely confirming Mr Tremayne's ownership of St Osyth Priory. Allegra might object to the plan, saying it was unfair to Miss Tremayne, that he was starting his married life based on a lie. No, let her believe, as Demelza must, that it was a love match. Much simpler that way.

★ ★ ★

The doors to the Grand Salon were open; they were dining in style tonight. Allegra had decided that she owed it to herself, and Richard, to show the Priory at its best. So she had ordered three courses and dozens of removes, to be accompanied by the best their cellar could offer. She had also arranged for champagne to be served before dinner. She rather felt they would all need it if the evening was not be an unmitigated disaster.

She need not have worried. Demelza, lovely in a simple gown of white silk with a silver gauze overdress, her hair piled on her head, black ringlets artfully escaping to frame her face, looked entirely at ease in her imposing surroundings. Tremayne, stern in black, his cravat a masterpiece, his single diamond pin magnificent, appeared equally unfazed by the formality.

Whatever their shortcomings, Allegra was forced to accept that they knew how to go on in society. Even Miss Murrell had risen to the occasion and her evening gown of deep purple, with a full turban liberally festooned with handsome ostrich feathers and diamante, looked every inch the *grande dame*.

Yardley served the champagne himself, a great honour, if only the newcomers had realized it, and by the time he announced dinner the assembled company were predisposed to enjoy themselves. Richard offered to escort Demelza who, with a happy smile, willingly rested her hand on his arm. Tremayne turned to Allegra.

'Would you permit me to escort you in to dinner, Lady Allegra?'

'Thank you, sir, that is most kind, but I prefer to come with Miss Murrell.'

His jaw clenched, but he hid his annoyance well.

She wished her thoughtless words unspoken but it was too late to undo them. She would endeavour to be charming over dinner to make up for her lapse. The meal, served *à la français*, the dishes placed down the centre of the table, the men serving the ladies with whatever they required, passed without

79

further mishap or embarrassments.

Richard was on sparkling form, putting himself out to charm. Demelza was captivated; her experience of men was non-existent; she had no yardstick to compare him with. In her eyes he was a godlike figure, and she could hardly believe that all his attention seemed to be directed at her.

When Allegra led the ladies back to the drawing-room she smiled slightly at her new friend.

'Lady Allegra, I wish to thank you for the gowns you sent me. I have never possessed such garments. But I feel like Cinderella, I believe that at midnight I will turn back into the dull schoolgirl I used to be.'

'Fustian, Miss Tremayne; you are a lovely young lady. The clothes merely enhance what God has given you in abundance.'

'Thank you, Lady Allegra. You're so beautiful, like a true princess. And you and Lord Witherton are so alike.'

Allegra smiled. 'We are twins, remember.' She hesitated; should she warn the girl about Richard's reputation? She heard the sound of male laughter and the moment was gone. She glanced up and found herself trapped by the intensity of Tremayne's gaze. Her head spun and she felt an unexpected flood of heat.

She stood up. 'Pray excuse me, everyone, I

feel a trifle indisposed and I must return to my room.'

Miss Murrell jumped up. 'I shall escort you, my dear. No, do not argue, I am coming. I do not wish you to collapse on the stairs.'

Tremayne bowed. 'I need to speak to you, Lady Allegra. Would you join me in the library before you break your fast tomorrow?'

She nodded. 'Will nine o'clock be convenient?'

'I shall look forward to it. Good evening, my lady.'

As she walked slowly back through the dark passageways and cavernous rooms, her arm linked firmly with Miss Murrell's, she pondered what possible reason Mr Tremayne could have for wishing to speak to her alone.

6

Demelza's eyes widened, then she giggled. 'I do not believe it, Lord Witherton; you're telling me Banbury stories.'

Richard clutched his hands to his chest and schooled his expression to one of astonishment. 'You shock me, Miss Tremayne! How can you reside here if you do not believe in St Osyth?'

'Of course I do, but not the part where she is decapitated by a Viking and picks up her head and carries it under her arm to this building before falling to the ground.'

Solemn faced, he pointed to the brown marks on the rough stone walls. 'Not even when you see her bloody fingerprints over there?'

She walked over to peer closely at the smudges. 'Inconclusive evidence, my lord. But I am sure St Osyth was a very devout princess and was indeed martyred for her faith.' She stared round, her face serious. 'I love the atmosphere in here. It is wonderful to think that this vaulted ceiling and these windows have been here for centuries. That we are standing on the flagstones where countless others through history have stood.'

He looked round with renewed interest, seeing the antiquity of the old monastery refectory through fresh eyes. 'You are right, Miss Tremayne. It is a privilege to be here. Having grown up in these hallowed surroundings I am afraid that I tend to take them for granted.' He smiled, finding his young companion delightful company. 'You must speak to Lady Allegra, she is the family historian. She will be able to tell you everything you could possibly wish to know about our ancestors and this place.'

She shivered, her muslin day dress too thin.

'You are cold, Miss Tremayne. Let us go out into the garden, it is warmer out there.'

The temperature was considerably more clement outside. 'Can we walk around the Priory before we go in to breakfast, Lord Witherton? I should like to view the ancient gatehouse again — it is a shame that the gates remain permanently closed.'

'It is indeed. The small doors you can see are still in use; our factor and the vicar live in the accommodation either side, and they use the small door to one side. Shall we go and look? I am entirely at your disposal, Miss Tremayne.' He offered his arm and she slipped her hand through, revelling in the contact. They strolled in silence for a while.

'My lord, may I speak frankly? I wish to ask a question that I am almost sure is impertinent.'

He hid his amusement. 'I promise I shall not be offended. Ask your question without fear.'

She stopped and stared up at him earnestly. 'If you and Lady Allegra love this place so much, why did you sell it to my father?'

He was too surprised by her question to answer. He should be angry, give her a sharp set down, but her innocence, the genuine concern he saw on her face, stopped him.

'My father gamed the place away. Mr Tremayne merely bought up his debts. We had no inkling of the situation until two days ago.'

'How dreadful for you! What a horrible shock it must have been.' He could see her eyes glittering with unshed tears.

'It is not so bad, Miss Tremayne. Your father allowed us to stay here to grieve in peace for nine months and when we have to leave, in two weeks' time, we are taking the family jewels. They will supply us with a more than adequate income.'

'It is not right. Withertons have lived here for hundreds of years. We are the interlopers. I shall never be happy here, knowing our

84

arrival has displaced you and Lady Allegra.'

He patted her hand. 'Thank you for your concern, my dear Miss Tremayne, but it is unnecessary, I assure you. We shall manage very well.'

'No, I shall not allow it.' She snatched her hands from his and turned away, too overcome to speak.

Strangely he found himself wishing to gather her into his arms, to stroke the dark curls and offer her comfort. He did not like to see her upset. He reached out, intending to touch her shoulder, but she spun back, her expression almost fierce.

'I have a solution to your problem. I wish you to promise you will listen and not interrupt.' She cocked her head, waiting. He nodded, giving her the courage to continue. 'My lord, if you were to marry me, your difficulties would be solved. You and Lady Allegra could remain here, where you belong. But also, I could live here without feeling guilty. I know that what I am suggesting is outrageous, but I am being practical. Tremaynes are famous for it.'

Richard had listened to her suggestion with mixed emotions. His initial shock at her presumption was immediately replaced by an unexpected feeling of affection for the earnest young lady staring up at him. He did not suspect for a moment that the offer was made out of self-interest, that she shared her father's desire for her to be a countess. She was prepared to sacrifice herself to save him. His throat clogged and his voice was gruff when he finally managed to answer.

'My dearest girl — I am overwhelmed by your offer — but I cannot allow you to do it. You do not know me; we have been acquainted scarcely a day. You are offering to tie yourself to me for life.'

To his astonishment she threw herself into his arms, allowing him no time to step aside. Before he realized what was happening he had encircled her waist and his mouth captured hers in a gentle explorative kiss. Who was the more shaken by the embrace it was hard to tell.

After far longer than was decent, he reluctantly released her but retained his hold on her hands. He gazed, entranced, at her sparkling eyes and swollen lips and he felt an unexpected constriction in his chest. Without conscious thought he dropped dramatically to one knee.

'My darling Demelza, will you do me the honour of becoming my countess?'

'Yes, please.'

He jumped up but, as he was about to enfold her a second time, he became uncomfortably aware that they were the centre of attention. Word had spread and several interested spectators were now gathered to watch him make a spectacle of himself and Miss Tremayne.

'Sweetheart, I think it best if we go in; we appear to have gathered an audience.'

Demelza glanced round, unconcerned, and smiled suddenly at the gawping gardeners. 'Good; now I am thoroughly compromised Papa will have to agree.'

'Hoyden! Have you no shame?'

'None at all,' she giggled. 'I suppose you must speak to my father, ask his permission to address me?'

Richard felt his cheeks colour and hastily took her arm to cover his embarrassment. 'Indeed I must, and it would seem to be a matter of some urgency to do so.'

They parted under the magnificent oriel windows that dominated the face of the ancient section of the Priory. She ran upstairs to share her news, in a letter, to her bosom bow, Lucy Carstairs. All thought of breaking her fast forgotten in her excitement. Lucy would be so jealous that she had not been the first to find herself a husband.

Demelza felt as if she had stepped into the pages of one of her favourite romance novels. She was the beautiful heroine, swept off her feet by a handsome prince, to live her life, happily ever after, in a castle. Admittedly, Lord Witherton, was only an earl but he was as handsome as any prince — indeed a great deal better looking than the overweight Regent she had once seen a picture of in *Ackerman's Repository* — and her intended did live in a castle. Well, almost a castle, and if it only had two towers and a gatehouse at least it was ancient. All heroes dwelt in ancient houses, of that, she was quite certain.

She ran her tongue along her still tingling lips and a delicious warmth radiated throughout her limbs. Lucy would hardly credit the news that scarcely three weeks after leaving the hated seminary for ever, she had become affianced to an earl and received her first real kiss.

She picked up her skirts and twirled around, laughing out loud with happiness. When finally exhausted and giddy she ceased, it was to find two young footman grinning at her quite rudely. She had not noticed them at their task of removing one of the dark-brown portraits from the wall of the blue gallery. She chose to ignore them, stalking past, with her nose in the air, wishing she could vanish between a crack in the polished floorboards.

★   ★   ★

Richard paused outside the study, took a deep steadying breath, and knocked over loudly.

'Enter.'

Richard did as he was bid, but his eagerness to share his good news with Mr Tremayne was somewhat diminished by that brusque command.

'Ah, Witherton, how can I be of assistance?' Richard was not invited to be seated.

'I have come to ask your permission to address Miss Tremayne.'

'The devil you have! Good God, man, you have only known her five minutes.'

'It is long enough, sir, to know that our affections are engaged.' Richard felt sick. This was not how the interview was supposed to go. He hurried on, hoping to remove the look of disapproval from his future father-in-law's features. 'In fact, sir, I have already asked Miss Tremayne to marry me and she has done me the honour of accepting.'

Tremayne's basilisk glare did not bode well. His silence was unnerving. Richard stumbled on, 'This is what you wanted, sir, what we agreed. I cannot understand why you look so grim. This is good news, surely?'

Tremayne slowly pushed back his chair and strode round to stand barely a yard away. Richard had to restrain himself from backing away; he would not allow himself to be intimidated. He straightened his shoulders and tilted his head to stare directly at Tremayne, refusing to give ground.

'I hardly think such a precipitate move is good news, but I'm prepared to be convinced. Explain yourself, Witherton.'

So it was that Richard found himself giving an account of what had taken place. When he finished Tremayne shook his head as if baffled. Then he laughed and the tension between them vanished.

'She is the image of her mother, you know, Witherton, but is like me in personality. I, too, make impulsive decisions, but I have never lived to regret them; let us hope my daughter does not do so either.'

The threat behind his jovial words was not lost on Richard. 'I have already given you my word that I will not let you down, sir; I believe that I am more than ready to take on the mantle of responsibility that marriage entails.'

'I'm glad to hear that. However I'm not giving my permission now; I wish to think about it. No, don't look so dispirited; I'm not saying no, after all it was my idea to forge a union between you in the first place. All I'm saying is that I will not allow your betrothal to be official until I'm sure Demelza is happy.'

Richard nodded. 'Very well, sir. I can understand your reservations. How long will you require to make this decision?'

Tremayne shrugged. 'I shall extend your departure date until the middle of May. At that point I shall either ask you to leave or confirm your engagement to my daughter.'

'Thank you, Mr Tremayne. Are you going to explain matters to Miss Tremayne, or shall I?'

'I shall. See that you do not overstep the bounds of propriety. I do not wish my daughter's reputation damaged in any way. I hope that I make myself clear?'

Richard fingered his neck cloth nervously. 'Yes, sir. I shall leave you to your papers. Pray excuse me.'

He was visibly shaking when he left the study. He dreaded to imagine his next encounter with Tremayne, when it became clear that his passionate embrace, the only aspect of the morning's events he had refrained from sharing, had been witnessed by half the outdoor staff.

He needed to clear his head, sort out his strategy for dealing with Demelza's formidable father. If he couldn't meet him without quaking like a *blanc-manger* he could imagine what his life would be like in the future. He would have to go cap in hand for every penny, be for ever begging his pardon and asking his permission. He knew he could not live like that.

If this marriage was to be successful, or even go ahead, it was up to him to prove that he was not a bacon-brained Johnny Raw, but a competent young man, well able to manage his estates and provide for a wife and family.

★　★　★

Allegra, from her sitting-room window, watched him bounding across the turf of the inner courtyard to the stables. Something, or someone, had obviously disturbed him. She looked at the mantel clock; it was time for her appointment in the library with Mr Tremayne. She was also intending to ride out as soon as she was free and was smartly attired in a royal-blue habit of military design, a jaunty feathered hat pinned securely to her hair.

With her gloves and whip in one hand and her skirts held up in the other, she hurried down for her meeting. The library door was open but, unlike her brother, she had no intention of knocking when entering any room in the Priory. It was *her* home until she left, whatever the legalities of the matter.

Tremayne was waiting for her. 'Good morning, Lady Allegra, I have a document I would like to read to you.'

'I presume it is on the same subject as my brother's?'

Surprised she should be so sanguine about such a sensitive issue he nodded. 'Yes, it is. Would you care to be seated?'

'No, thank you, I am not staying. Please give me the paper; I am quite capable of reading it for myself.'

She held out a hand, and her direct bright blue gaze held him captive. Mesmerized, he picked up the parchment and placed it on her palm. He felt the prickle of heat surge up his arm as he deliberately allowed his hand to brush against hers. He felt her flinch at the contact and watched her draw back her arm as if burnt.

'I take it you require me to sign this in front of Mr Evans?' He nodded. 'What time is he expected, sir?'

'At noon.'

'Then I shall return, with the document fully scrutinized, at that time. Now I am going to ride down to the creek; it is too fine a day to remain indoors.'

She was unaware of the impact her brief visit had made but was only too conscious that the hand that he had touched still felt unpleasantly hot, as if she had placed it too close to the fire.

In the hall she spotted the butler. 'Yardley, have this taken up to my apartment.'

'Yes, my lady. Will you require a luncheon to be served today?'

'I shall breakfast when I return, but if neither Miss Murrell nor Miss Tremayne come down before noon then, yes, have a cold collation served.'

The gallop across the marshes, her long-suffering groom struggling to keep pace, added colour to her cheeks and gave her the appetite she needed before facing any meal. She ate sparingly, as usual, and her plate was half full when she left the table.

Richard met her in the hall. 'I have been searching for you, Allegra. I must talk to you. Come into the small drawing-room, we can be private there.' She followed him, knowing whatever was bothering him was about to be revealed.

'Well, Richard, tell me what is troubling you?'

'Nothing. I am to be congratulated. I have asked Demelza to marry me and she has accepted.'

Stunned, she reached out gripping a convenient chair back. 'Good heavens, you have only known her for a day? How can you be so . . . so foolhardy?'

He smiled, glad she had issued such a mild rebuke. 'I love her. I knew it the moment I set eyes on her and she feels the same way.'

'But she is little more than a child — what can she know about love between two adults?'

'She is seventeen; many girls are married even younger. I consider her age no drawback.'

'Have you spoken to Mr Tremayne?'

'Of course I have, he is happy, in principle, but will not give his permission for our engagement to become official until the middle of next month.' Now would have been a good time to reveal the true state of affairs, but Richard had begun to believe his own rhetoric and almost forgotten his initial reason for courting Miss Tremayne.

'I see. But we are to leave here in two weeks . . . '

'No, we are to stay until he has decided. If he agrees then we stay, obviously; if not, we leave.'

'In which case, Richard, I shall also reserve judgement. I wish you to be happy, and if Miss Tremayne is essential to achieve this end, so be it. I shall offer no objections if her father gives his permission. She is a charming girl. Not what I would have chosen, but you will not be the first man to marry out of his station when his affections are engaged.' She carefully refrained from mentioning money: it would be too vulgar.

He grinned. 'Thank you. I am content with that. You wait and see, Allegra, you will realize very soon that Demelza and I are meant for each other.'

They embraced fondly and she resumed her journey upstairs. Before changing she spied the roll of parchment awaiting her attention. She supposed she had better read it, although she already believed she knew its contents. Tossing her hat, gloves and whip carelessly on to a chair she removed the ribbon and unrolled the document.

She scanned the neatly scribed words and after a few lines her stomach somersaulted and for a minute she forgot to breathe. The words danced before her horrified eyes. She read again, refusing to accept what she saw. How dare he? How could he suggest such a *mésalliance*?

She recalled her unkind words to Captain Pledger. Was she being punished for her cruelty? Being made to marry, not quite from the stable, but almost as bad. She felt a suffocating pressure on her chest and perspiration beaded her forehead. Her heart began to race and she believed she was dying, suffering an apoplexy. She closed her eyes and prayed, asking God's forgiveness and waited for death to claim her.

However, as she relaxed, her pulse steadied and the weight lifted, and slowly she regained her faculties, was able to open her eyes. Was she being granted a miracle? Being spared for some higher purpose? As oxygen returned to her system the effects of her panic receded and her brain began to function more rationally. She appreciated that her sudden illness was a result of shock and her recovery a natural progression, and no divine intervention had been involved.

Smiling a little at her fantastical imagination she sat considering the import of what she had read. There was something moving just outside her understanding, something she knew was relevant, but she could not quite grasp it. Then she did.

She sat bolt upright. Good heavens! When she had told Tremayne she knew the contents of the document as it was similar to Richard's he had looked surprised. Of course he had! Her brother had, for the first time in his life, deceived her. He had lied about the agreement; it would appear that he was also being coerced into marriage. How could he pretend to love the poor child? Was he so desperate to save his heritage and provide for his sister, that he would marry without love?

She leant back and closed her eyes again, trying to marshal her chaotic thoughts. Her father had killed himself rather than live without the Priory, so marrying to save it was surely a better option?

Was this why Tremayne was withholding his permission, did it all depend on her? She read the rest and discovered she was right. If she refused to marry him then Richard could not have Demelza. Were they both to be sacrificed for the sake of their heritage? She sighed, then so be it. She could not allow Richard to be the only one to suffer.

Idly she scanned the last paragraph. Her mouth curved. She had not taken Tremayne to be a stupid man but this clause proved she was incorrect. She had her escape. It was going to be easy to force him to retract his offer. All she had to do was appear even colder, haughtier and treat him with disdain and contempt. He was a proud man; he would surely refuse to marry her, however much he desired her, if he knew that she despised him.

She smiled mischievously. And if that failed, she could arrange to have him taken by the press gang. One way or another she would make sure he was not at the ceremony. Knowing she would never actually be forced to share his bed, she was quite content to go downstairs and sign the man's wretched document.

She paused, then picked up the parchment and reread the clause, to confirm she had it clear. Yes, it did state that if any party failed to turn up on the date specified for the wedding, things would change. If a Tremayne reneged, the estate would be returned, intact and free from mortgage, to Richard. If a Humphry did so, they would be forced to leave the Priory, penniless, without even the family jewels.

Reassured, she walked towards her bed-chamber where Abbott waited to help her wash and change. She was still puzzled that Richard believed he had to pretend he was in love with Miss Tremayne. Anyway, all that was irrelevant, they would have the estate back and neither of them would be obliged to make the ultimate sacrifice. The possibility that she might be the only one of the four people involved who felt this way did not occur to her.

7

'Papa, I have explained how it was. I offered for Lord Witherton first.'

'But why, Demelza? If you agree to marry Witherton you will not have a season. I had already arranged for you to be sent vouchers for Almack's and they were not easy to come by I can assure you.'

'I should have hated it, Papa. All that simpering and curtsying, knowing everyone thinks me vulgar and only there because you have bribed a patroness.'

His eyes widened. 'Good God! How do you know about such things? You have only been out of the seminary a few weeks.'

She giggled. 'It was the main topic of conversation, or one of them. Don't you see, I was never part of the inner circle; that was reserved for the titled and wellborn girls regardless of their financial status. Lucy and I were tolerated because of our enormous wealth and so learned all about the rules and expectations of the *haut ton*, and also the names and ranks of all the eligible *partis* available this season.'

He stared at his daughter. She might be

only seventeen but she was wise beyond her years. 'So you would know about Witherton?'

'No, he was never mentioned. I imagine it was because he has been out of Town for more than a year.' She smiled winningly at her father. 'You will give your permission for Lord Witherton and I to become betrothed?'

'No, not yet. I have told him you must spend more time together, get to know each other better, and if after four weeks you're both of the same mind then you shall have my blessing.'

She opened her mouth to protest but saw the set of his jaw and decided against it. 'We shall not change our minds, Papa. We are in love. Although it can affect a person instantly it does not make it any less durable than a love that grows over time.'

He laughed. 'You are right, my dear. But remember that I shall expect you to behave with decorum at all times. You will not walk out with Witherton again unchaperoned, is that understood?'

She dropped her head, feeling her face suffuse with guilty colour. 'Of course. May we ride out together?'

'Yes; however I would prefer it if Lady Allegra were to accompany you. Otherwise Miss Murrell must be at your side.'

He watched his only child hurry from the

room, obviously agitated. Was she hiding something from him? He rang the bell, waiting impatiently for a footman to appear. 'Ask Miss Murrell to join me here.'

He walked back and forth the library, deep in thought. It was turning out to be a morning for surprises and he was not overly fond of them. He heard light footsteps heading towards him and knew that Lady Allegra's middle-aged companion was arriving.

'Pray come in, Miss Murrell. Take a seat.'

Miss Murrell subsided on to a chair, her plum-coloured, heavy damask gown settling around her neatly shod feet. 'How can I be of service, sir?'

He nodded. Sensible woman — she did not prevaricate. 'I would like to ask you to be Miss Tremayne's companion. Would you be prepared to take the position if Lady Allegra is agreeable?'

'Lady Allegra has already spoken to me about such a possibility. As she is now five and twenty she considers that she no longer needs a chaperon, but she is wrong. Unmarried ladies always require a female companion. It is expected.'

He was confused. 'Are you saying that you are not available to take on Miss Tremayne as well?'

Miss Murrell beamed. 'No, Mr Tremayne. I shall be delighted to act in that capacity for your daughter, as long as you realize my first duty is to Lady Allegra. I have been here since she was a little girl. I was companion to the countess first.'

'That is acceptable. I must take you into my confidence, Miss Murrell. Lord Witherton and my daughter wish to become affianced. I have told them they must wait until the middle of May for my decision. I wish them to be chaperoned at all times until then.'

'Naturally you do, sir. A young lady's reputation is to be protected like precious jewels.'

'I'm glad we understand each other. I'm sure you do not wish to discuss remuneration with me. I shall have Mr Evans talk to you later, if that's acceptable?'

Miss Murrell rose, and curtsied politely. 'Thank you, Mr Tremayne. That is most considerate of you. I have arranged for the mantua-maker to come from Colchester this morning. She is an excellent seamstress and makes all Lady Allegra's gowns. Although the gowns Miss Tremayne has been given fit very well they are somewhat outmoded. A young lady in her position should be *á la mode*, as I am sure you would agree, sir. So, if you will excuse me?'

Tremayne stared out off the window his brow creased. How could he have been so thoughtless as to place his daughter in the position of having to borrow garments? He should have noticed Demelza was unfashionably dressed, that she had only her school apparel to wear.

He must have seemed a careless parent to both Witherton and Lady Allegra, dressed as he was in the best Weston could supply and his own child obliged to appear in secondhand clothes. The fact that these garments had an impeccable provenance did not make it any easier to accept.

Then his lips curved. Lady Allegra had noticed his omission and had unobtrusively stepped in and did what was necessary. Underneath her brittle exterior she had a kind heart. He had chosen well; she would make him an excellent wife and would, God willing, become a good friend to Demelza.

For the greater part of ten years he had lived alone, had had no one with whom to share his thoughts and plans. The young woman he had decided to marry was intelligent and he relished the notion of spending the rest of his life in her company. His life would never be dull, of that he was sure.

But would she acquiesce to his demand?

Did she love her brother enough to put his happiness before her own? It was a gamble — but then his fortune had been built on taking risks. He had never lost and did not intend to do so now, even if it meant employing less than honourable tactics to achieve his goal.

He pulled out his pocket-watch and glanced at it; an hour yet before his appointment with Lady Allegra. Time enough to write a letter to his mistress, Camille, breaking off their association. He had no further use for the voluptuous widow of Sir James Oliver. He had enjoyed what she had given but had paid well for it.

Lady Oliver had received thousands of pounds in gifts and jewellery in exchange for her favours. She was still attractive; would no doubt soon find another male protector. He sharpened his quill and dipped it into the well. He frowned. How much should he give her as a severance gift? Disgusted he threw the pen aside, sprinkling the pristine sheet with ugly black blots.

He could not bear to write to the woman, to sully the atmosphere of the Priory with such a venal letter. No, Evans must take care of it. He could send Lady Oliver a bank draft for one thousand pounds and make it quite plain he had no further interest in her. He sat back, stretching out his booted legs, and closed his eyes letting his mind fill with the image of the ethereal beauty he intended to marry. He knew he would remain celibate until the day that Lady Allegra became his wife.

If anyone had told him that Lady Oliver had hoped to fill that role he would have been astonished. He had never considered her any less of a commodity than all the other goods he bought and sold. He believed that the letter and the money would be the end of the affair.

★　★　★

Abbot held up a third afternoon dress for Lady Allegra's inspection — this one with an eau-de-nil figured silk skirt and demi train and deeper, almost turquoise, closely fitting beaded bodice. It was a dress for making morning calls, or receiving them, not staying at home. But it was not Abbot's place to say so.

Allegra wrinkled her nose. She wished to create a certain impression and the selection of the dress was crucial. She wanted to emphasize her assets, but still appear aloof. Her lips curled as she realized she did not have many *assets* to show. Since her father's death she had lost so much weight it was hard to distinguish her front from her back.

She pointed to the eau-de-nil. 'That one, please. I know it's for more formal occasions, but it is imperative that I make a good impression this morning. All our livelihoods could depend upon it.'

'In which case, my lady, you have made the right choice. You will certainly impress any gentleman wearing this gown.'

'Excellent. I think I shall wear my pearls and the pendant ear-bobs.'

'Shall I thread some through your hair as well, my lady?'

Allegra nodded. 'I have less than thirty minutes before I have to be downstairs. It is a great shame to waste my bath but I have no time to enjoy it. Today my ablutions must be quick.'

She was ready to go down, the document in her hand, only a few minutes past the appointed time. She paused in the hall to study herself in the huge gilt glass hanging over the mantelshelf. The milky pearls coiled around her neck were a perfect complement to the elegant simplicity of her gown.

Her heart thudded uncomfortably inside the restriction of the fitted bodice, but she was not certain if she was apprehensive or excited by the forthcoming encounter with

Mr Tremayne. She had decided to give him the impression that she was resigned to the matter, but that it was not a union she could like. If she appeared too sanguine, he might suspect her motives.

The library door, as before, stood open but this time she could hear the murmur of male voices. She swept in, head high, and both occupants were rendered speechless. She saw Tremayne's teeth clench and his eyes darken with passion and her pulse quickened. She was going to enjoy this confrontation; when a man's interest was aroused it was so much easier to achieve one's aims.

She tossed the parchment on the desk. 'If Mr Evans is ready to witness my signature then I am ready to sign.'

The lawyer checked the quill was sharp, unfastened the ribbon and smoothed out the document. Tremayne remained silent. 'If you would be so kind as to sign here, my lady, and here.' Allegra did so with a flourish. She watched Evans sign then shake sand over the writing.

'Thank you, Mr Evans. If your work is done here I bid you good day.'

Tremayne nodded his consent and the lawyer hastily collected his hat and cane. However, when he reached for the agreement, Tremayne shook his head. 'No, leave it,

I wish to keep the document in my possession. Thank you for your assistance in this matter. I'll be in touch. Good day, Mr Evans.'

The silence thickened. He waiting; she rehearsing her part. It was going to be more difficult that she had anticipated. She had thought that staying aloof from him, after all he was far beneath her touch, would be an easy task. But for some inexplicable reason, each time she saw him, her concentration faltered and her breathing became erratic.

He was a formidable opponent — he emanated a strength of will, an implacable authority that she had never encountered before. She stiffened her spine. She must not let him intimidate her, or all would be lost. All she had to remember was that she would rather remain a spinster than marry a man as common as he, however rich and personable.

'Mr Tremayne, there are certain facts that I must make clear to you.'

He indicated that she be seated but didn't answer. When she was settled he perched on the edge of the desk, his face impassive, his eyes watchful. For a second Allegra felt she was making a grave error, but ruthlessly repressed the thought.

'I have signed your vulgar document because I have no choice. I do not wish my brother to lose his heritage and I have no desire to spend the rest of my life a pauper.' She shrugged and raised her eyebrows. 'I believe that I have the best of the bargain, Mr Tremayne. I shall be able to stay here, in my ancestral home, close to my brother. But I am not what you think, sir.'

'What is that, my lady? I should be interested to hear.' His rich baritone sent unlooked for shivers down her back.

'I am not interested in anything apart from the Priory, my brother, and the well-being of my staff. There is no room in my heart for anything else.' She risked a glance and her breath stopped in her chest. He was smiling; laughing at her! How dare he? It was insupportable.

All her carefully planned words were forgotten as she was propelled to her feet by her indignation. 'You find me a matter of amusement, sir? Your arrogance leaves me almost speechless.' She treated him to a thorough inspection from the top of his dark head to the toes of his polished Hessians.

She met his navy eyes, her own icy. 'I admit you are a fine-looking man. I would have to be blind not to see that, but it is a total irrelevance. You are so far beneath me that even as rich and as handsome as you are, you can never reach me.' She had his full attention and he was no longer finding the situation amusing. 'Good, I believe we understand each other. It is best, I think, to go into such a marriage of convenience with one's eyes fully open. If you expect nothing then you are not going to be disappointed.'

She nodded, as if to a servant, and prepared to leave. He stepped forward, preventing her. She could feel his body heat, almost hear his heart pounding. She had to move back, place a safe distance between them, but his hands reached out and grabbed her arms, his fingers biting into her.

'I think, my dear, that your understanding of the situation is as far from the mark as it is possible to be.'

She gulped, her bravado evaporating — she was unused to being manhandled. 'Please, sir, release me. You are hurting my arms.' Her response was so unexpected, and so quiet, that he instantly did as she requested.

Allegra rubbed her upper arms, her face pale, for the first time in her life unsure what to do. Should she reprimand him? Demand an apology, or leave in disarray? The decision was made for her.

'I apologize most sincerely, my lady. I had no intention of hurting you. I merely wished to prevent you from leaving before we had completed our conversation.'

'May I leave now, Mr Tremayne? I am feeling unwell.'

'Of course. Shall I call your abigail?'

'No, thank you. I need no assistance.' She fled from the library, not sure to whom the honours had gone. She needed to walk outside in the cool of the Wilderness; allow her emotions to calm, let her intellect take control. As she paced along the shady path her hectic colour began to fade. By the time she completed the walk she was more composed.

Allegra wandered into the rose garden and sank on to a marble bench, the cool stones pleasant beneath her hands. Her lids closed and she leant back, allowing the midday sun to soothe her. She relived the interview, trying to discover at what point he had gained the ascendancy. She smiled, and her eyes flew open. He had won the battle when she had lost her temper. It was simple; in future she must keep a tight hold on herself, not allow his arrogance, or patronage, to rouse her.

It was imperative that she maintain her composure. She frowned. What was she thinking? She did not have a quick or fiery temper. She was renowned for her coolness; even as a child her brother had been unable to dent her *sang froid*.

What was it about that obnoxious individual that caused her to behave so? Her reverie was rudely interrupted by the sound of hasty feet and someone calling her name. What disaster had befallen them now? She stood up, instinctively smoothing down her skirts and turned, a friendly smile fixed to her face.

'Miss Tremayne, I do hope there is nothing amiss?'

8

'Oh, Lady Allegra, I do beg your pardon for disturbing you. Shall I go away? Really I do not mind in the slightest.'

'I am delighted to see you, Miss Tremayne. How can I be of assistance?'

Demelza's shoulders slumped and her eyes filled with tears. 'My Papa will not allow me to become betrothed to Lord Witherton until the middle of next month. I do not know how I shall bear it.'

'Sit down, my dear, and tell me what has transpired. I had no inkling your affections were so soon engaged, for after all you have only known my brother since yesterday.'

'Indeed I have, my lady. But we knew as soon as our eyes met. It was a *coup de foudre*! I know you are going to explain to me that I am too young to make such a decision, but even Papa knows that I'm already a sensible adult lady, quite able to make up my mind on such matters.'

Allegra was not convinced. 'And Witherton, does he feel the same urgency to be wed?'

'Oh yes, he does. We know we are destined

to be together. What need do I have for a season in Town when I have met my true love?' The girl shifted miserably on the bench. 'We're not even to be allowed to be alone together, but must somehow still get better acquainted. How do we do that? And four weeks is so long.'

'My dear, it would be impossible to hold a ball, or party, for your betrothal until we are out of mourning and that is not until July, you know,' Allegra told her kindly.

Demelza's mouth rounded with horror. 'Oh dear, I do apologize. How stupid of me to forget. I do not wish for a long engagement, neither does his lordship. But we could be married in August, could we not?'

'If Mr Tremayne is agreeable then there is no reason why not. But do not be in too much of a rush, Miss Tremayne. On reflection you might discover that you and Witherton do not suit. Once you are married, it is too late to repine. Are you quite certain that you wish to spend the next fifty years living here, at St Osyth's Priory?'

Demelza shook her head, her black ringlets dancing around her elfin face. 'I do not intend to languish here all year round. There is a townhouse and I intend to spend the season there. And as soon as this horrible war is over I shall insist that we take a grand tour.

Papa has a yacht, you know.'

Her ingenuous remarks could not cause offence. Allegra stretched out and took a small hand in hers. 'And when there are children, my dear? Shall you still wish to gad about, abandon them here to the care of their nanny and nurse-maids?'

'Children?' Demelza looked shocked. 'I do not wish to have children, not for many years. I am fond of babies, but I am too young to have any of my own.'

Allegra hesitated; should she explain to this naive and innocent girl just what married life entailed? That babies were usually an inevitable result of sharing one's bed with one's spouse. 'Of course you are, my dear; there is plenty of time to consider filling your nursery.'

'I know it will be my duty to provide an heir for Lord Witherton one day, but that will be, I hope, a long time in the future.'

Allegra stood up, shaking out her skirts. 'I believe I can see Miss Murrell approaching, Miss Tremayne. Shall we walk to meet her?'

They strolled back side by side through the budding rose bushes, Demelza chatting of this and that. No more was said about the responsibilities of marriage, but Allegra had grave misgivings about the girl's readiness for such a step. She would have to have a long and serious talk to her brother before things moved on to the point where they could not be reversed.

The fact that both Richard and Miss Tremayne declared themselves to be in love only complicated matters. It put her in an invidious position. If she forced Mr Tremayne to withdraw then it was unlikely in the extreme that he would then consent to his daughter's nuptials.

'Miss Murrell, were you looking for us?' Allegra asked as they met.

'Mrs Dawkins is here from Colchester, my lady, for Miss Tremayne.'

Demelza skipped forward, her face alight with anticipation. 'I'm coming at once, dear Miss Murrell. I can't wait to select my new gowns.' She turned to Allegra. 'It is not to say that I do not love your gowns, Lady Allegra, especially this one. Primrose is almost my favourite colour.'

'Run along, Miss Tremayne. It will take a while for your new gowns to be assembled so it is fortuitous that you like the ones that I gave you, is it not?'

Demelza smiled. 'And anyway, Lucy always says that a young lady cannot have too many gowns, so expect I shall need to keep all of them, including yours.'

Allegra's brow puckered as she watched

them depart. In her opinion Miss Tremayne was still far too young to contemplate marriage and she was even more determined to inform her brother of her feelings on this matter.

She decided to walk across the Bury to the church. She felt the need for the solace that only quiet communion with her Maker could bring. Inside the ancient building it was unpleasantly chill but the myriad colours, thrown into fragmented patterns on the rough stone floor by the sun streaming through the stained-glass windows, made up for the cold.

She knelt before the altar and tried to compose a prayer but her head was full of unchristian thoughts. Full of schemes to force Tremayne to break the contract and give her back her home and freedom. She shivered and scrambled to her feet not finding the peace she sought. She would be better back in the Priory, in her own apartment where it was warm. With her companion occupied today with overseeing Miss Tremayne's new clothes she could be sure of privacy.

★ ★ ★

Allegra dismissed her maid and curled up in the window seat that overlooked the lawn.

This gave her an uninterrupted view of the ancient gatehouse, and the flock of shaggy sheep that grazed there awaiting the attentions of the shearers. She needed to think more carefully about her notion to alienate Tremayne to such a degree that he would wish her to perdition.

He was not a man to be easily manipulated. For, a commoner he was unnecessarily proud and highhanded, more so than he had any right to be. Wealth was not the equal of good breeding — blood-lines were paramount in her opinion.

As she gazed, unfocused, through the leaded panes, some movement over by the bailiff's house caught her attention. She stared at the two men she could see talking in the shadow of the building. One was Fred, an under-groom, the other obviously a sailor, dressed as he was in navy serge and thick woollen sweater. The men parted after shaking hands and Allegra surmised that contraband had played a part in the discussion. Being so close to the coast, smuggling was a way of life.

Free-traders! Perhaps that was the answer to her problem. She jumped from the window seat and grabbed the bell, ringing it loudly. Abbott appeared, her expression anxious.

'I wish to change my gown; I need a

walking dress for I am going to visit the stables.'

'Would you like to eat some luncheon before you go, my lady? You had no breakfast this morning.'

Allegra was about to refuse, but Abbot looked so worried she relented. 'Very well. Perhaps broth, and some fresh bread and a piece of fruit?'

Changed into a less formal, but equally elegant, peach cambric frock, with matching spencer, soft brown, kid halfboots on her feet, Allegra felt more disposed to tackle the food which was waiting on the side table in her withdrawing-room.

Her appetite was, as usual, meagre but she managed to swallow enough to satisfy her abigail. 'I shall return in good time to dress for dinner. The gold Indian silk will be suitable for tonight, Abbott.'

Allegra, knowing she might well be observed from the study window, forced herself to appear nonchalant, suppressing her urge to hurry. She had formulated a plan and was eager to set it in motion. Once through the arch that led to the stables she felt it safe to lengthen her stride. Tremayne could not possibly observe her progress now.

The stable yard was quiet, as was to be expected in mid-afternoon. However, Thomas was sitting outside the tackroom, a side-saddle draped over his knees, making it impossible for him to perform the required bow so he touched his forelock instead.

'Please do not stop your work, Thomas.' These were the first words she had spoken directly to him since the unfortunate incident on the day the old earl died. Somehow the fact that her head groom had been obliged to put his arms on her person no longer seemed such a breach of etiquette.

'I wish to speak to Fred, is he about?'

Thomas shook his head. 'No, my lady. He just left for the smithy with Billy; two carriage horses needed shoes. They'll be back before dark.'

Did Thomas have contact with the local free-traders? Should she risk involving him? The matter was taken from her hands.

'Ah! Lady Allegra! I saw you disappear into the stable yard and was intrigued.' She remained silent, her face impassive. Tremayne continued apparently unbothered by her lack of civility. 'It is rather late to be contemplating a drive, but if you have urgent business please allow me to escort you.' He stopped, waiting expectantly for her response. Even Thomas was watching, his head cocked, waiting to see what she would say.

Through tight lips she replied, 'I wished to

speak to a member of staff but as he is not here I shall continue my constitutional.' She nodded at Thomas. 'Thank you, Thomas. Please ask Fred to come and see me when he returns.' Allegra tilted her aristocratic nose in the air and stalked off, giving Tremayne the cut direct.

★　★　★

Thomas suddenly became absorbed in his tack cleaning, hoping his hunched form was somehow invisible. Mr Tremayne's face was a study. He heard his new master swear impressively, under his breath, before striding off. It wasn't like Lady Allegra to be so rude, but the situation must be difficult. After all they were about to be thrown out of their ancestral home.

He sat back, his brow creased. Why did Lady Allegra want to see Fred? He was an under-groom, had no direct dealings with the folk at the Priory. It was a mystery and no mistake. He spat noisily on to the leather saddle and continued his polishing. It was no business of his; he was not going to get involved. He was just happy the mistress was no longer ignoring him.

★　★　★

Allegra would have had to be as deaf as a trunk maker not to hear her name roared across the lawn. How vulgar to shout in such a way! Believing that this lack of manners now put her on the moral high ground she halted, turning slowly and stood, commendably patient but strangely nervous, waiting for Tremayne to reach her.

His expression was ominous, his intention obvious. Too late she decided to relinquish her precarious position and assume a more conciliatory mode.

'Lady Allegra.' He stopped a scant arm's-length from her, his breathing agitated but his voice steady. 'Lady Allegra,' he repeated softly, 'I believe, pray correct me if I am mistaken, that you failed to answer my question.'

Thoroughly unnerved and reduced to incoherence by his unnecessary proximity, Allegra clutched her hands to her chest and stepped back. Maybe she would be able to marshal her scattered wits and find her voice if the distance between them was greater.

Alas, as she retreated, he followed, unmoved by her distress. Soft footed he prowled after her, determined to get his answer. Answer? She had forgotten his question. She stopped so abruptly he cannoned into her knocking the remaining breath from her lungs.

She swayed backwards, her arms flailing wildly, and her fingers finally lodged in the froth of his stock. She hung on, hoping his substantial weight would be enough keep her on her feet and thus save them both from an unpleasant and undignified tumble.

They teetered, back and forth, as Tremayne fought for his balance and his breath. Regaining both he raised his hands and placed them, none too gently, over hers.

'Let go, you're throttling me. I promise you're not going to fall.'

Allegra was unable to respond. Her fingers remained clawlike at his throat and lightly he prised them from their stranglehold. Her heart pounded unpleasantly and her vision remained blurred. Nothing seemed to make sense. Finally she registered the fact that Tremayne was holding her hands captive in his; that she was far too close to his solid flesh for comfort or indeed, decency.

'Lady Allegra, look at me.' His voice was soft and she could not refuse. 'That's better. If you are fully recovered I'm going to release you now.' She nodded, still too shocked to speak. 'There, I apologize for my appalling clumsiness. It could have had us both over.'

'No, sir; it was entirely my fault.' Her words, once unstoppered from her throat gushed out. 'I should not have been so uncivil. I should have answered your kind offer. I am not usually so rag-mannered, I do assure you.'

As she spoke she had not dared to raise her eyes but now she did. 'Good heavens! Whatever has happened to your neck-cloth, Mr Tremayne?' Her puzzled enquiry, for some inexplicable reason, reduced him to whoops of laughter. Although flustered, and not a little embarrassed at such a display in public, she did not withdraw.

After several noisy minutes he wiped his eyes and grinned down at her. 'My dear girl, you did this to me! You mangled my stock and ruined my valet's assiduous efforts to turn me out as a gentleman.'

'I did it? Are you sure, sir? I have no recollection of . . . ' Her voice trailed away as she remembered grasping something crisp but pliable to prevent her fall. She felt the colour travel swiftly from her toes to the crown of her head.

'Quite so. But I do assure you, Lady Allegra, that your misguided attempt at strangulation shall not be a bone of contention between us in the future.'

'Strangulation?' She shook her head in frustration and stepped back to give him a fulminating stare. 'It is not a matter for merriment, sir. A real gentleman would not have mentioned it.'

All traces of humour vanished and he was once again the autocratic, overbearing stranger, the one she was to be forced to marry if she did not take steps to prevent it. She would not apologize a second time. Being forced to do so once was more than enough. From the depths of her silk-lined bonnet she glared back at him, daring him to retaliate.

The impact of his formal bow was somewhat reduced by the flapping ends of his destroyed neck-cloth. 'If you have no wish of my services as an escort I will bid you good afternoon, Lady Allegra. No doubt we will meet at dinner.' He did not make it sound as though he relished the prospect. 'Dinner will be at seven o'clock in future. I have no intention of keeping country hours.'

She knew it would be pointless to protest that dinner was always served at five o'clock at the Priory. He was now the owner and he could choose when and where they were to eat. She inclined her head a barely discernible fraction, but did not honour him with a reply.

Whatever time he wished to dine, she would eat in her rooms at five o'clock as usual and she would suggest that Richard dined with the officers at Weeley. Even without Captain Pledger as his escort, there were sure to be several gentleman there who would be only too pleased to vouch for him.

★ ★ ★

Allegra pushed away her tray, the turbot with lobster and cucumbers in white sauce barely touched. 'I am going downstairs. I sincerely hope that man will be elsewhere. I have no desire to see him again today.'

'Very well, my lady. Will you be requiring anything else to eat tonight?' Abbot stared pointedly at the rejected food.

'Have some bread and cheese, and a slice of Cook's plum cake sent up for supper.' Allegra reached out and selected a carefully peeled and cored slice of pineapple, fresh from the orangery. 'I shall eat this before I go out, but you must send the rest back.'

She stood by the window and saw her brother striding off towards the stables. He turned and waved knowing intuitively that his twin was watching him. Smiling, she returned the gesture, glad she had persuaded him to dine elsewhere. She had intended to confront him with his duplicity; ask him why he was pretending to be enamoured with Miss Tremayne when she knew that he was constrained to marry her by the document he had signed. But the moment had not been opportune. He had been so exhilarated, so excited and, apparently, in spite of the evidence against it, so besotted with his future fiancée that she hadn't the heart to destroy his happiness, however ephemeral it might prove to be.

His affections could not possibly be genuine, not after such a short passage of time. It was, no doubt, another of his starts. She smiled as she recalled him, years ago, professing his undying love for a comely serving girl at the local hostelry, but he had soon got over that.

Miss Tremayne was not a village girl, she was a lady. His account of their embrace had been shocking, but as long as it was not repeated, it should not have caused any lasting harm. At least this was one subject on which she and Mr Tremayne were in agreement: Richard and Demelza must be chaperoned by herself, or Miss Murrell, at all times.

It was obvious if this *mésalliance* was to be prevented, it was she who would have to arrange for it to fail. Richard would, naturally, be grateful once he was free of his obligation and could resume his carefree bachelor existence.

The pineapple, although juicy and sweet, no longer interested her. She cast the uneaten part back on to the tray and quickly wiped her sticky fingers. She glanced at the clock — a little before six — with luck the Tremaynes, and Miss Murrell, would be safe in their rooms dressing for dinner. Still in her walking dress, she stole through the long corridors and down the plain wooden stairway preoccupied by thoughts of how she was going to explain her outrageous plan to Fred.

It was one thing to decide that the solution to her dilemma was to remove Mr Tremayne from the vicinity, but quite another to ask an under-groom, however loyal, to arrange for him to be kidnapped and sent to France in the care of the local smugglers.

9

London, May 1812

The ballroom was a crush, hardly surprising for one of the last fashionable occasions of the season. Lord and Lady Harborough always held their ball in the middle of May, as a grand finale, before the *ton* began to retire to their country estates for the summer.

Captain Gideon Pledger, in scarlet regimentals, attracted several simpering smiles from hopeful debutantes as he threaded his way through the crowd that skirted all the main reception rooms, but he ignored them.

He had been summoned to Horse Guards that morning where he had been told that he was to report for duty in June. On his return to his lodgings in Albemarle Street that afternoon, he had found a letter from a brother officer stationed at Weeley. The news it contained had not been happy.

Witherton, it appeared, was now betrothed to the Tremayne chit and the wedding set to take place in August. He had no objection to this; marrying a cit's daughter to restore one's fortune was perfectly acceptable. It had been the second item that had raised his choler and sent him into the stuffy, over-crowded Harborough residence to seek out the one person who could possibly help him.

Lady Oliver was, as expected, surrounded by a bevy of hopeful would-be protectors. The captain had anticipated this and had his note written. He signalled to a passing footman and watched his missive being carried across the room.

The recipient read it and glanced up, nodding in his direction. Message understood. He shouldered his way through the crowd towards the open French doors that led out on to the terrace. The warm May evening meant that overheated dancers could parade outside to cool down before returning to the fray. Here they could stroll, unre-marked, but remain private.

He did not have to wait long before his quarry arrived. His eyes narrowed in appreciation. She was a beauty; rounded in all the right places. But she did nothing for him. His nighttime fantasies were still filled with images of a tall, golden girl removed, for ever, from his reach. She was engaged to marry that rich bastard, Tremayne.

He bowed and offered his arm to Lady Oliver and she took it. He did not speak until they were safely away from the press of people around the doors.

'Thank you for responding so promptly to my note, Lady Oliver.'

'Is it true, Captain Pledger? Tremayne is to marry Witherton's sister?'

'Yes, it is a fact. There is to be a double celebration on the twelfth of August. They are all but lost to us now.' He felt her fingers clench on his arm. 'But I have a proposition to put if you are prepared to listen.'

'Go on. It will do no harm to hear what you suggest.'

They paused by the balustrade, under the flickering light of several flambeaux. To a casual observer they were a couple, talking quietly, whilst admiring the vista of lawn and inhaling the scent of the jasmine and honeysuckle that rioted over the stone walls.

'Allegra shall not marry that man. If I cannot have her, then no one shall.' His voice was soft but it sent a chill down Camille's spine.

'What do you propose? Are you intending to murder her?' Her brittle laughter shattered the night air.

'That is exactly what I propose.' He felt her recoil. He gripped harder and prevented her escape. 'Come now, my lady, what is she to you? Merely an obstacle in the way of what you most desire. With her removal, Tremayne will return to you. You shall have what you want.'

She felt sick. She desperately wanted Silas back, had discovered that no other man would do, but murder? Had she the stomach for that? 'Is there no other way?'

'This will be the easiest. You will not be personally involved. You need to know nothing of the matter until it is over. All I require from you is the wherewithal to finance it. My pockets are to let.'

'But she is so young and — '

He interrupted her, his voice hard. 'She is a cold-hearted, proud bitch. The world will not miss her, I can assure you. Are you part of this or not?'

She was undecided. Killing someone, however much they were in your way, was such a drastic step. 'I am not sure.'

He dropped her arm and stepped away, shrugging. 'No matter. I can as well dispatch both as one.'

'Not Silas? Oh no, you cannot. I thought I hated him for his callous rejection, but I find that I still love him. I do not want him dead.'

His mouth curled in an empty smile. 'In that case, help me, and I will spare him.'

He gave her no choice. If sacrificing an unknown girl in exchange for her lover was the price, then she would pay it. 'Very well.

How much do you require for this unpleasant venture?'

He named a sum that made her gasp. 'That much?'

'Loyalty does not come cheap, my lady. I have to select my accomplices carefully.'

'I shall have the money ready for you by the end of next week. I shall have to sell some jewellery in order to raise such a large amount.'

'There is no immediate urgency. I will send my man round; there is no need for us to meet again. When the matter is completed, believe me, the whole world will be talking of it.'

Pledger bowed and sauntered off, to vanish back into the brightly lit reception room. Lady Oliver remained outside a while longer, composing herself; it would not do to appear in anyway discommoded by her stroll. The town tabbies' censorious eyes were ever watchful.

When she swept back in to rejoin the party her smile was radiant, her eyes sparkled and her ruby-red ball-gown swirled enticingly around her neatly turned ankles. As the circle of admirers enveloped her once more, her co-conspirator joined the hardened gamblers in a side-room set aside for that purpose.

Captain Pledger felt lucky. He had snared Lady Oliver in his web with consummate ease and anticipated being able to dip into that particular honey-pot again and again. Blackmail was always a lucrative business. A man must, after all, provide for himself the wherewithal for luxuries by whatever means he could.

St Osyth Priory

'Are you run mad, Allegra? What are you thinking of?' Richard viewed his sister with horror. 'I have no wish to break off my betrothal to Demelza. I love her. No, do not pucker up like that, my dear girl, I am speaking the truth.'

'That is flummery, Richard. You are marrying Miss Tremayne to line your pockets. You signed a similar document to mine so you cannot pull the wool over my eyes with your protestations of true love.'

'That was six weeks ago. Things have changed. Good God, Allegra, you must see how things are between us now? It is you who have been making yourself as disagreeable as possible. I tell you, that if you were my intended, I would tan your backside and bring you smartly into line.'

She shrugged, indifferent. 'Anyway that scheme has failed dismally. Whatever I have tried he has remained unmoved.' She shivered a little as she recalled the final encounter. She had known then, what she had suspected all along, that Tremayne was not a man to be trifled with.

He had threatened to turn off all the Priory pensioners, one by one, if she continued with her campaign of incivility. Unless she behaved as she ought she had no doubt that he would carry out his threat. She could not allow that and abandoned her first plan and treated him with due cordiality. With that he appeared content.

She returned to the matter under discussion. 'Am I to take it that you do not wish me to tell Miss Tremayne about your gambling and the string of ladybirds you kept in Colchester and Town? You do not wish me to try and give her a disgust of you?'

'Absolutely not! Such knowledge is not suitable for a young girl. And I have mended my ways, you know I have. I am a reformed man.'

She raised one eyebrow. 'Visiting the officers' mess at Weeley and returning in your cups is reformed, is it?'

Richard grinned. 'I said I had given up women and gaming, not drinking. Come on,

Sis, a man must be allowed to retain one vice, surely?'

'Ah — but one can so easily lead to another, Richard. Before you realize you could be back in Colchester, or London, indulging in every imaginable form of debauchery.' She was struggling to keep her lips from quivering. Her brother rose so easily to the bait.

'Dammit all, Allegra, I am not a rakehell!' he replied testily. Her gurgle of laughter finally alerted him.

★　★　★

The sound of their laughter travelled along the hollow, dark-panelled corridor, from the morning-room to the study where Tremayne was, as usual, working on a pressing business matter. His austere features softened but his eyes were sad. Why did he only hear Allegra's happiness from a distance? These past few days she had been civility itself, her manners impeccable, but she rarely smiled and never laughed when in his company.

He was beginning to have grave doubts about the wisdom of forcing her to the altar. Should he withdraw his offer? Give back the Priory and put his massive expenditure down to experience? Endure a failed business deal for the first time in his life?

He stood up, slamming his chair back, his face determined. He would not give up; it was a matter of principle. Silas Tremayne never lost. He would have to approach the problem from a different angle. He had, so far, given his fiancée free rein, made no demands. From now on things would be on his terms. What she would not yield freely, he would take. His accounts could wait — Allegra's education could not.

He strode towards the morning-room eager to begin his campaign. Two blond heads turned as one; two pairs of gentian-blue eyes rounded in surprise, but only one mouth curved in a welcoming smile.

'Good morning, sir; I was about to seek you out. I wish to inform you that Demelza and I are going over to Great Bentley. There is a fair on the green today and Lady Arabella Grierson, who resides in the hall, has invited us to spend the day with them.'

'What time are you planning to leave on this excursion?'

'As soon as Demelza is ready.' Richard smiled ruefully. 'Which could be any time between now and noon.'

Tremayne turned to Allegra. 'I wish to visit the fair with you. We shall take the barouche.' He nodded at Richard. 'No doubt you will wish to drive that abominable contraption of yours?'

'My high-perch phaeton? Demelza loves it. I would not dare suggest we travel any other way.'

Allegra had listened to this jocular exchange with rising agitation. She had no desire to spend a day in Tremayne's company. For some reason the more time they were together, the harder she was finding it to remain aloof. When they had been waging a war of words it had been simple, her emotional barriers had been easy to maintain, but now she was obliged to be civil, it was different. He was urbane, relaxed and his natural charm sometimes made her forget how much she hated him.

'I am sorry, sir, I cannot accompany you. I have an aversion to country fairs. Too much noise and jostling, quite unacceptable.'

It was Richard's turn to stare. 'That is fustian, Allegra. You love them. It is always you that has to be persuaded to leave.'

She flushed painfully and glared at her indiscreet brother. 'That was a while ago. I have matured since then. And I find I no longer wish to go.'

'Witherton, go and see if my daughter is ready; inform her that we are leaving in thirty minutes and she will be left behind if she is not down.' Tremayne waited until they were alone before responding to her mendacious statement.

'Lady Allegra, do you wish to change from that enchanting confection, or will you accompany me dressed as you are?'

Her nostrils flared and her lips compressed. 'My gown is immaterial, sir, as I am not coming.'

He moved slowly in her direction and she forced herself to remain immobile, praying he would not come too close. She was unaccountably flustered when he did so. He halted, a short arm's-length, from her. His expression friendly, his eyes more so. She found herself relaxing, returning his smile. He spoke, his tone gentle.

'You are coming to Great Bentley, my dear, willing or not. You will be ready, at the door, at the appointed time or I shall seek you out and bring you by force. I am sure you would not wish to make a spectacle of yourself in that way.' He remained, a slight smile playing on his lips, apparently at ease, but ready to move fast if necessary.

She gazed at him for a moment, too shocked to answer. Her colour drained away and she swayed slightly. That was his cue to act. He closed the gap between them and before she could protest she was cradled in his arms, her feet dangling above the floor. 'My dear, you are unwell. I apologize for my high-handed behaviour. I will carry you to your rooms forthwith.' He pulled her closer, crushing her against his solid chest.

Finally she found her voice. 'Put me down this instant, sir. I am not unwell and you know it.'

'Are you not, my dear? I was certain you were about to swoon. You went so pale.' His voice was bland, but his rock-hard arms remained firmly around her. Allegra thanked God he was no longer moving towards the door.

'I insist that you release me, Tremayne. This instant.' Her words were forced out from behind clenched teeth. If she could just get a hand free she would box his ears soundly.

'I will set you down if you agree to come to Great Bentley.' He gave her a little shake, his tone affectionate. 'You will enjoy a day out, you goose; it is far too long since you had an outing of any sort.'

She had no choice. 'Oh, very well, if I must. But, I promise you, sir, I shall not enjoy it. I am determined to have a miserable time.'

He restored her to her feet but did not relinquish her arms. 'Look at me, Allegra.' Reluctantly she raised her head. 'Playtime is over, sweetheart. It is time to accept that our union is inevitable and begin to appreciate the advantages of such a match and not dwell on the negative aspects.'

Her throat constricted and words would not come. Unexpectedly her eyes filled. He made her feel so vulnerable, helpless, and she hated it.

'Do not cry; I did not mean to distress you.' He tugged softly and she found herself gathered into the warm security of his embrace.

Tremayne felt his blood surging through his veins and it took all his willpower to do no more than hold her loosely for a second, when he wanted to crush her, feel her female outline imprinted against his. He dropped his arms and she stepped back hastily.

Allegra smiled up, believing she was secure in her victory. He reached out and brushed his thumb across her mouth, enjoying her involuntary reaction. 'Are you going to change? You do not have long to do so, if you are.'

She barely restrained the urge to stamp her feet in frustration. 'I am still to come? I thought you had relented.'

'No, my lady, I did not relent, I merely sympathized.' He bowed, and his dark eyes flashed a message she could not fail to understand, and she was alone, her emotions in total disarray.

She ran lightly upstairs to put on her bonnet and collect her matching parasol and reticule. A moment's mischief prompted her to insist that both Abbot and Miss Murrell accompany them. As both couples were betrothed, and they were intending to travel in an open carriage, a chaperon was unnecessary. She knew Tremayne would be furious and that almost made up for the fact that he had taken the honours in their latest confrontation.

At the appointed time the ladies were assembled on the lawn. Richard's phaeton, drawn by two pairs of perfectly matched bay geldings, arrived first. His tiger jumped down from his perch at the rear of the carriage and ran round to hold the horses' heads.

'This is a glorious day for an outing, Allegra, so try not to look so prune-faced about it, there's a good girl.' Richard's shouted comment was heard by everyone in the vicinity, including Tremayne, standing quietly behind the ladies.

Allegra wished the ground would open up and swallow her and she was obliged to hide her scarlet face behind her parasol. Demelza smothered her giggles behind her hand and Miss Murrell pretended not to have heard. Tremayne was not so tactful.

'Oh, come now, Witherton, prune-faced?

143

That is doing it rather too brown. I would say that Lady Allegra might look a little blue-devilled, but no more than that.'

This had the desired effect. Allegra's mortification turned instantly to ire. Her head shot up and her colour faded leaving just two patches across her cheekbones. She was forced to keep her pithy reply to herself as Richard dismounted and tossed Demelza up on to her seat. He sprang up beside her, the horses were released, the tiger scrambled back to his place and the phaeton left in a flurry of gravel.

Tremayne settled his party comfortably in the barouche then stepped back, slamming the door. It was only then Allegra realized he had had no intention of travelling in the carriage with her. He was riding his magnificent black stallion. He touched his hat and waved them off impervious to her dagger stare. She could hear his laughter following them.

By the time the barouche had left the park she was more ready to enjoy the outing. She sat back, closing her parasol with a decided snap. She stared out of the open carriage. The verges were lush green, peppered with the bright yellow of cowslips. She closed her eyes for a moment to listen. 'Can you hear any nightingales, Miss Murrell? That was a cuckoo, I am sure of it.'

'I do believe you are right, my dear. But it is hard to tell if the nightingales are singing because there are so many other birds doing the same.'

Allegra finally relaxed. 'I did not wish to come today, but Mr Tremayne insisted.' She paused, but Miss Murrell made no comment. 'But I rather think I am glad to be here. It must be three years since I attended a fair at Great Bentley. I find I am looking forward to it.'

'Of course you are, my lady. It is a lovely summer's day and you are going to spend it in good company.'

The carriage bowled along the lane, passing pedestrians and pony traps filled with villagers also intent on spending a day at the fair. Their passage slowed as they turned into the lane that led to Great Bentley for they were forced to follow behind several like-minded carriages. These events were famous throughout the area and anyone who had time to spare, and pennies to spend, made an effort to attend.

There was a clatter of hoofbeats alongside and Tremayne appeared. He handled his spirited mount with consummate ease. 'I shall ride ahead. Apollo needs to stretch his legs.' He smiled directly at Allegra and her heart

145

turned over. She watched him urge his horse through a gap in the hedge, her expression a little bemused. Miss Murrell interrupted her reverie.

'My dear Lady Allegra, I am so glad you are finally becoming reconciled to your marriage. That your reservations about Mr Tremayne are over and your affections engaged.'

All pleasure in the excursion evaporated. Allegra froze her companion with a stare. 'Miss Murrell, I think that you forget yourself.'

She watched the middle-aged lady shrivel, her kindly face pinched with hurt and wished her angry words unspoken. The shock of hearing that in Miss Murrell's opinion she held a *tendre* for *that man* had caused her to speak harshly.

Her companion was far out in her assumptions. There was no rapport between them. He desired her, nothing softer motivated him and she held him in complete dislike. She sat stiffly against the squabs endeavouring to force the image of a pair of penetrating navy eyes, and a devastating smile, firmly from her mind. She did not want to marry Tremayne; it would be an intolerable *mésalliance*. But she had no alternative. She was trapped. All joy in the day vanished and she squeezed back unwanted tears.

She groped in her reticule for a handkerchief and, with head bowed, she surreptitiously wiped her eyes. It was no good — she had to accept the inevitable — at least married to a wealthy man she would lack for nothing. Richard's nuptials could not go forward if she refused. She was not so sunk in selfishness that she could ruin her brother's life to benefit herself. Acceptance of the situation brought with it a kind of peace and Allegra felt ready to enjoy the day again. She turned to Miss Murrell.

'I sincerely apologize for my unspeakable rudeness. I am not sleeping well, but it is no excuse, I know. I pray that you can forgive me for I do not wish to ruin today.'

'I accept your apology, Lady Allegra. Let us say no more about it.'

But Allegra knew she had mortally offended her dear friend and that it would take more than a few words to restore harmony between them.

10

The journey continued in uncomfortable silence, Allegra gazing raptly at the cow parsley bobbing and curtsying, its frothy cream flowers dramatic against the darker green leaves of the hawthorn hedge. Miss Murrell was equally entranced by the same scene unfolding on the far side of the carriage. Abbott sat opposite them wishing she had been left behind to get on with her mending.

'This is quite ridiculous, Miss Murrell. We have been friends for ever and however uncivil I have been, it is your Christian duty to forgive me.' This speech was delivered to the back of her companion's best chip-straw bonnet. 'Do not stay up in the boughs, please; we shall both have a wretched day if you do.'

Slowly the bonnet turned revealing a far from happy face. 'I have said that I accept your apology, my lady; however, I wish to point out to you that since Mr Tremayne and dear Miss Demelza came to reside at the Priory, I believe you have changed. I scarcely recognize you as the dear girl I used to teach.'

Allegra's jaw dropped. 'I had no idea I had

become so objectionable to everyone. It is only Mr Tremayne that I dislike. I have become fond of Miss Tremayne over the past few weeks. After all she is to be my sister soon.'

Miss Murrell sniffed and pursed her lips. 'And you are to become her mama, have you thought of that? The child is neither blind nor stupid. She cannot be enjoying the constant friction between her father and yourself.'

'You are quite correct to admonish me, my dear friend. I have behaved appallingly. I have allowed my own feelings to overcome what is acceptable. I promise it shall not happen again.' Her companion looked unconvinced, believing that this *volte face* was too sudden to be genuine.

Allegra leant forward to add emphasis to her plea. 'I am, like my brother, a reformed character. From this point forward I shall be a pattern card of civility. The most conciliatory of fiancées. I give you my word; there will be no further unpleasantness between us.'

'I am so pleased to hear you say so. I shall indeed say no more for your further actions will demonstrate your sincerity, will they not?'

Allegra sat back, satisfied she had gone a long way to repairing the relationship. Her lips curved up as she contemplated spending a day with the newly married Griersons.

Charles and Lady Arabella were well known to her, and although not close she was eagerly anticipating having a female nearer to her own age to converse with.

She frowned as something occurred to her. Would Tremayne expect to dance attendance on her all day? She sincerely hoped not. There were bound to be cock fights, and possibly a horse race or two, to occupy him.

It took a further forty minutes for the barouche to travel the last mile to Great Bentley but Allegra had not been bored. She had smiled and waved to dozens of acquaintances and been seriously ogled by three society gentleman recently arrived from London.

Lord and Lady Hawksmith, Lady Arabella's doting parents, were famous for the splendour of their summer house-parties. From Bromley Hall it was but a short drive to Great Bentley so it was quite possible these top-of-the-trees gentlemen were staying there. Although the season had not quite finished many of the *haut ton* would have already closed up their Town houses and left to enjoy their summer in the fresher atmosphere of the countryside.

Allegra glanced down — glad she had decided to keep on the eau-de-nil walking dress that Tremayne had admired. Abbott reached out and adjusted the bow that secured the matching silk-lined bonnet.

'There, you look lovely, my lady. It's no wonder all the gentlemen are staring.'

It had been so long since she had felt the warmth of admiration and approval from the opposite sex. Allegra felt her face soften, her smile become genuine and the pain and worry of the past years began to slip away. She knew she was going to enjoy this outing in spite of her initial reservations and her semi-serious threat to Tremayne to hate every minute.

'Oh look, my lady, Lord Witherton and Miss Demelza are already here. That is his lordship's phaeton being led away.'

There was no sign of Apollo. Either Tremayne had not arrived, or he was also inside the smart mansion making his bow to their hosts. The groom appeared to hold their horses and a footman emerged from the handsome front door and ran down the marble steps. He skidded to a halt beside them and opened the carriage door with a flourish.

Allegra descended first, her back straight, her parasol furled. She waited for Miss Murrell to join her then they strolled in to the house, puzzled that neither their host nor hostess was on the step to greet them.

'Where is everyone, my lady? I know that Mr Grierson and Lady Arabella are newly wed but surely they are aware that to leave invited guests to enter unannounced is the height of discourtesy?'

'I agree, it is decidedly odd.' She turned to the waiting footman. 'Conduct us to Lady Arabella and Mr Grierson, if you please.'

'They are in the garden, my lady.'

The footman led them across the chequered floor looking decidedly uncomfortable, obviously realizing that this was a serious breach of etiquette.

'Abbott, I shall not require you. If you wish to return to the Priory then ask Thomas to take you back.'

Abbott beamed. 'Oh no, my lady. I should like to visit my sister who lives on the green. What time do you wish me to return here?'

'Be back here by four o'clock. Enjoy your day, Abbott.' On impulse, Allegra dipped into her reticule and removed a silver coin and slipped it into Abbott's palm. Then she followed the smartly liveried young man as he took them through the house and out on to the terrace. 'Good heavens! Whatever is going on over there?' She saw, on the far side of the lawn, her missing hosts, plus Demelza and Tremayne, staring up into the canopy of a large chestnut tree. Of Richard there was no sign.

The young man paused, keeping his face

admirably impassive. 'I believe that her ladyship's cat is stuck up the tree, my lady, and Lord Witherton is attempting to rescue it.'

The two ladies scampered across the expanse of newly scythed greensward eager to join in the fun. Tremayne heard them approaching.

'Welcome. As you see we have a daring rescue under way. Unfortunately as Witherton ascends so does the wretched feline.' He directed their attention to the uppermost branches.

'Richard is an excellent climber of trees. There is not one of any size in our demesne that he has not conquered at some time during his formative years.'

Tremayne grinned, his teeth of flash of white. 'I sincerely hope you're correct, my dear. It is a long way to fall from there.'

She shuddered dramatically. 'Do not even think that, sir!' She craned her neck to watch the delicate proceedings unworried by her brother's valiant efforts. She felt her bonnet begin to slide backwards and hastily straightened her head. 'At least that explains why we arrived ungreeted. But I am sure that they must have an extremely efficient staff here; where are the housekeeper and butler, I wonder?'

'I understand they have the day off, as do most of the servants, to attend the fair.' Seeing her startled look he added, his eyes twinkling, 'I know, shocking, is it not? But the cook has prepared a magnificent cold collation, I'm told, for our nuncheon. Also there are parlour-maids and footmen to attend us, should we have need of them.'

Demelza, hearing Allegra, spun round her face contorted with anxiety. 'I am fearful that he will fall, my lady. I know he will. He should not have gone. It is only a wretched cat, why should he risk his life for that?'

'Do not fret so, my dear.' She handed the girl her kerchief. 'Now, dry your eyes, you do not wish them to be all red and puffy when he returns, do you?'

Tremayne stepped up and slid his arm around his daughter's shoulders. 'Lady Allegra is quite correct, my love. It is far more likely the cat will fall than Witherton.'

This comment was overheard by Lady Arabella, already beside herself with worry for her beloved pet. She collapsed, wailing, into the arms of her husband. By the time Charles had soothed his overwrought young wife and Tremayne and Allegra had restored Demelza to some degree of equanimity, Richard was beginning his descent. He had the errant cat tucked firmly inside his waistcoat.

'I am coming down now, so you can all relax. The cat and I are safe,' he called through the branches. Instantly the waiting group looked up. This time Allegra remembered to place a restraining hand on the back of her bonnet. She noticed that Demelza's hat was hanging, unheeded, from its ribbons, halfway down her back.

Lady Arabella was not wearing a bonnet. In fact, Allegra noticed with some amusement, she was still in her morning gown, a plain cotton dimity not intended to be seen in company. Richard had completed over half his climb, the small black head of the cat just visible under his chin, when there was an ominous cracking and the narrow branch upon which he had just placed his right foot, gave way.

Demelza screamed, her cry so startling, the cat shot upwards, attempting to claw its way across Richard's unprotected face. Allegra held her breath and instinctively moved closer to Tremayne, but he was gone, no longer beside her.

Assessing the situation he had leapt forward, tearing off his jacket as he did so. 'Hang on, lad, I am coming up.'

Allegra watched, aghast, as he climbed rapidly, as adroit in the branches as her brother, until he was able to support

Richard's dangling feet.

'Stand on my shoulders. I am firmly braced below you. Regain your balance before trying for another foothold.'

Richard braced himself, then gently tried to remove the terrified cat from its position, crouched on top of his head. But the cat was not prepared to co-operate and with an angry yowl, it clawed Richard a second time and he was forced to release it.

To gasps of horror, the unfortunate animal plummeted to the ground. It landed, as cats do, on all fours, shook itself, and shot off hissing and spitting in the direction of the house. Lady Arabella was the first to react.

'Well, after all the trouble that has been taken to rescue him. What an ungrateful animal he is!' Amidst the laughter of relief the would-be rescuers emerged feet first from the tree. Tremayne dropped lithely to the ground but Richard fell heavily, sprawling face down on the grass. He rolled over, his hands clutched to his face, to be greeted by a further scream of anguish from his intended.

'Richard, you are covered in blood. That horrid cat has scratched you to ribbons.'

Tremayne dropped down on one knee and slipping his arm under Richard, he heaved him up to prop him against the tree trunk.

'Lean on that for moment, until you get your breath back.' Concerned at the amount of blood seeping through Richard's fingers he produced a voluminous handkerchief from his inside pocket and, folding it into a pad, carefully prised the hand away. 'Hold this on your eye, press firmly.'

Tremayne had deliberately kept himself between the injured man and the watching ladies. Without turning he spoke to Allegra. 'Allegra, take Demelza inside. I will deal with this.'

She didn't argue. 'Come along, Demelza, let us go in. Richard does not want you to see him so discommoded. You know what gentlemen are like about such things.'

She caught the eye of Charles, his arm still protectively around his wife. He understood the unspoken message. 'Arabella, sweetheart, shall we go in and find your naughty pet?'

Allegra glanced again at Tremayne. She mouthed the word 'doctor' and he nodded, his expression grim. She tightened her hold on the softly weeping girl and hurried her inside. She felt sick to her stomach. Something terrible had occurred. There was too much blood staining that white hand-kerchief for it to be a mere scratch.

Demelza was bundled into the morning-room and a parlour-maid left to attend her.

Lady Arabella ran off to look for her cat leaving Charles and Allegra to speak privately.

'I fear that Richard is gravely hurt, Charles. You must send for Dr Jones. As you know, he is usually stationed at the Lion, on days such as this.'

Charles nodded, his face pale. 'I should have gone up the tree myself. Then none of this would have happened.'

'Charles, you must not blame yourself. Accidents happen. Since you broke your leg so badly two years ago you know you are not able to climb trees. Richard or Tremayne had to climb, and Richard is far younger, so obviously it was he who volunteered.' Even as she spoke the words of comfort she was thinking that fetching a cat down from the tree should have been a job for a gardener's boy.

Charles sent a groom galloping across the park to fetch the doctor. The Lion Inn abutted the far boundary of Great Bentley Hall and could be reached by way of the churchyard. If Dr Jones was where they expected, he could be with them in a matter of minutes.

A footman had been organized to carry blankets and a parlour-maid to convey brandy and strong wine outside to Tremayne and the invalid. Allegra ran inside to get

158

directions to the kitchen where she could collect a jug of boiled water and some freshly washed cloths. Then she hurried back to do what she could for her injured brother.

Charles joined her at the French doors. 'Why has Mr Tremayne not brought Richard inside? He would be far more comfortable. I shall have the downstairs apartment made ready just in case it is needed.'

Allegra acknowledged his remark with a nod and hastened towards the two figures under the tree. Her brother was still sitting his back against the trunk, his legs stretched out in front of him. Tremayne knelt in front of him. She could not quite discern what he was doing.

As she approached, closely followed by the servants, she could hear Tremayne talking softly to Richard. 'You need to sit still, lad; hold a pad hard against your eye. The doctor will be with us soon.'

His eye? The cat had damaged Richard's eye by its frantic clawing. Maybe it was not as bad as she had feared. 'Mr Tremayne I have brought boiled water and clean cloths. I am quite able to deal with Richard's injuries. I am not missish — I will not swoon away at the sight of his blood.'

Tremayne straightened, patting Richard on the shoulder as he stepped back. He indicated that she should move with him until they were out of earshot of the patient. 'It is very serious, my dear. I fear Richard has lost his eye.'

Allegra almost dropped the items she was holding. He took them from her and handed them to Charles, standing silently, his face ashen, beside them. 'Take these over and put them beside Witherton. Drape the blankets over him and give him some brandy. Do not touch his face, or allow him to remove his hand. Is that clear?'

Charles nodded. 'Yes, sir.'

'Get on then. I'll be there in a minute.' He turned his attention back to Allegra. She tried to step round him, rush over to her twin, see the injury for herself. 'No, sweetheart, it is better if you do not see him now.'

'I must, please; he is my soul mate, my twin. We have always shared everything.' She tried to push past but he restrained her, enclosing her gently in his arms.

'He does not want you or Demelza to see him like this. He has told me so. Let me deal with it, please. It is for the best and it is what he wants.'

For a moment she continued to struggle. She caught her breath as a sob threatened to escape. Somehow she found herself enveloped in the arms of the man she believed she hated and despised. She rested her face against his shoulder allowing him to stroke her back; his hands tracing paths of comfort up and down her spine.

Shuddering she raised her head, her eyes awash. 'He will not die, will he? Please tell me he will not?'

He smiled and dropped a kiss on her parted lips before holding her at arm's length. 'Of course he will not die, you ninny. But he will be disfigured and very likely have the sight of only one eye.' Her tremulous smile almost unmanned him.

'As if I care about his looks. He is my dearest brother. If I can be sure he will not perish then I am happy to leave him in your capable hands and will retire to the house. Do you think the doctor will suggest that he stays here? Charles is having a downstairs apartment prepared at this very moment for that eventuality.'

'I'm certain it will not be safe to drive him home today.' He hesitated, then pulled her in to rest securely against his heart. Allegra, stunned by his unexpected action, parted her lips in bemusement, and gazed up at him, her eyes huge in her pale face.

He lowered his head, covering her mouth with his own. Allegra froze — for a moment it hung in the balance. Then her lips softened under his and she relaxed into his embrace with a sigh. They both forgot the parlous situation, the watching servants, and, unwisely he deepened the kiss. Allegra stiffened, jerking her head back in fright. Instantly he stepped away, removing his hands from her arms.

He bowed, his expression sincere. 'I most humbly apologize, Lady Allegra. That was an unforgivable lapse on my part.'

She stared at him, unsure how to reply. Then, unexpectedly, she smiled. 'We are both overwrought, sir. But as we are an engaged couple, I do not believe we have offended propriety in any way.'

His eyes blazed, his mouth curved and his smile was so powerful Allegra felt her stomach lurch in a decidedly peculiar way.

'Go in, sweetheart; there is nothing you can do here. This is going to be a difficult time for everyone.'

The sound of pounding feet caused them to look round. Dr Jones, bag in hand, was arriving, two footmen carrying a hurdle between them, bumping along behind.

Tremayne gave Allegra a gentle push in the direction of the Hall. 'Take care of things inside. Anything that can be done for your brother will be done.'

Reluctantly she did as she was bid. She

could hardly believe that in the space of a few minutes what had seemed to be an amusing incident had turned into a tragedy.

★　★　★

Cook had sent out runners to recall all the senior staff that could be found. The butler was now back inside to greet her.

'Lady Allegra, the housekeeper has taken Miss Tremayne to lie down. Lady Arabella and Miss Murrell have gone up with her. I have to inform you, Miss Grierson is here with Mr Edward. I have placed them in the small withdrawing-room.'

'Thank you. Please have some refreshments sent upstairs and also to the drawing-room.'

An attentive footman escorted Allegra to where the visitors were waiting. She was well acquainted with both Charles's younger brother and his oldest sister. Miss Grierson was standing, miserably twisting her hands, watching from her vantage point by the open window, the figures gathered under the chestnut tree. Of Edward there was no sign.

'Emily, what a time to meet again. Richard has severely injured his right eye, but his life is in no danger, merely his sight.'

'Allegra, how awful! For poor Richard to be so disfigured when he is so proud of his looks. I cannot bear to think of it.'

'Then, I pray you, do not. He has more than enough people worrying over him. Where is Edward? I was told he was in here with you.'

'He has gone out to the garden to see if he can be of any assistance.' Emily wiped her eyes. 'I can hardly credit that there has been a second serious accident in the space of two short years. Last time it was my dear brother Charles they bought in on a hurdle, this time it is yours.' She blew her nose noisily and mercifully stopped talking for a moment.

Allegra joined her at the window. She could see a sombre group carrying the prostrate figure of her brother. Even from here she could see the snow-white bandage covering his face. Dr Jones was walking on one side of the makeshift stretcher, Silas on the other. Charles was leading, his face serious, his limp more pronounced than usual.

'They are bringing Richard into the house. Please excuse me, Emily, I must go to him.'

It was as she hurried across the hall that she realized that not only Richard's life had changed. She was so astonished she stopped, shaking her head in disbelief. Somehow over the past few minutes she had stopped thinking of her betrothed as a man beneath her touch. He was no longer 'Tremayne', to her he had become 'her dearest Silas' and she, for some inexplicable reason, had fallen totally in love with him.

11

Allegra paused, not sure in which direction to go for Great Bentley Hall was a vast modern edifice and this her first visit. The property had been given to Charles on his marriage to Arabella in March, by his foster sister, Marianne, now the Countess of Wister.

She spied the butler crossing the hall and beckoned him over. 'Please conduct me to the rooms in which Lord Witherton is to be housed.'

The black-garbed gentleman bowed politely. 'They have prepared the ground-floor apartment, the one old Sir James used, my lady. I will take you, if you would care to follow me.'

She could hear voices as they rounded the corner. The rooms she sought were conveniently placed at the rear of the building, away from any bustle and having convenient access to the garden. Allegra hesitated at the doorway, not wishing to interfere in any way. The bedchamber door, which led from the large, airy sitting-room, was ajar, but she could not see what was happening inside.

She guessed that the footman would be placing Richard on the bed. She would not go in, not yet, not until Silas told her Richard was ready to receive visitors. She walked further into the room, not sure whether to sit or remain standing. She selected an upright wooden chair, with a padded seat, and perched on it. Scarcely two minutes had passed when, unable to keep still, she stood up and began anxiously pacing, back and forth, her half boots silent on the thick pile of the oriental carpet.

What was happening behind the door? Why didn't Silas come out to tell her how Richard was doing? She felt hollow — as if someone had reached in and scooped out her insides — making it impossible for her to breathe or swallow.

She halted in front of the French doors, her back to the bedroom, staring out over the garden. She wrapped her arms tightly around her middle as if attempting to console herself. She did not hear Tremayne's soft feet approaching.

His arms slid around her, pulling her close. He said nothing but his warmth, his strength, gave her the comfort she needed. She leant back, turning her face into the softness of his crumpled shirt, loving the experience of being held safe in the embrace of the man she loved.

Slowly her tension drained away and she

felt strong enough to turn, to study his face for the answer to the question she could not bring herself to ask. He met her enquiring gaze, his eyes filled with regret and she knew.

'Oh no! My poor Richard.'

'He will make a full recovery, but his eye cannot be saved. Doctor Jones is doing what he can to repair the damage. There will be scars, his face will no longer be a thing of beauty.' She felt his hands clench behind her. 'If I can lay my hands on the bloody animal I'll break its neck.'

He knew he should drop his hands, release her. But to his delight Allegra tentatively stretched up to run her fingers over his cheeks. He froze, not wishing to spoil the moment by a sudden, off-putting movement.

'You need a shave, Silas. I can feel the stubble of your beard.'

Slowly she traced the outline of his lips and he could remain still no longer. One hand moved up to cup her head the other pressed her so close that he could feel her soft contours against his heated body. Then her fingers travelled lightly round to link behind his neck, dragging his head down. Her eyes told him what he wanted to know. His mouth enveloped hers, his lips moving slowly, seductively. This time she responded; her newly discovered love giving her the courage to respond.

Her breasts were crushed against his chest and her feet were no longer on the floor. Then he placed her back on the carpet. Her legs were too weak to support her, and his arms remained around her. He feared she would crumble into a heap at his feet otherwise.

The texture of the cloth beneath Allegra's face was strange, not rough but soft. 'Silas, you have no jacket on. You are still in your shirt sleeves.'

'I am, my darling; I must apologize for having the temerity to kiss you improperly dressed.'

A gurgle of laughter greeted his dry comment. 'I do believe, sir, that you are dressed as befits the occasion. Improper behaviour does not require a jacket.' His smile sent further tremors through her limbs and she was obliged to clutch at his shirt front for support.

A discreet cough from just behind caused them to jump apart, but Tremayne kept his arm around her waist as they turned round to face the bedchamber door.

'My lady, sir, Lord Witherton is comfortable and asleep. I have given him laudanum to facilitate his rest and allow his body to recover from the trauma.'

'What is the prognosis, Dr Jones?' She was relieved her voice was firm.

'He has lost the sight in his right eye. I have done what I can to repair the damage but he will never see from it again, of that I am certain.'

'How badly is he disfigured?' Tremayne asked the question she had not dared to voice.

'The majority of the scratches are superficial and they will heal completely. However those around his right eye and cheek will not. Lord Witherton might feel more comfortable with a patch in future; that should cover up the worst.'

Allegra swallowed her gasp of horror. Tremayne's arm tightened protectively. 'Thank you, Dr Jones. My brother is a strong man; he will not allow this to ruin his life. When will we be able to move him, take him back to the Priory?'

The doctor's brow furrowed. 'If he does not develop a fever overnight then I should think it will be safe to move him tomorrow or the next day. I will reassess the situation when I return in the morning.'

Charles had emerged from the sickroom as the doctor concluded his speech. He waited quietly until the butler escorted the physician out. 'Mrs Blake, my housekeeper, is willing to act as nurse. But Richard has made it abundantly clear that he does not wish either you, Allegra, or Miss Tremayne, to be involved in his care.'

'He is right, my love; you take Demelza home. I shall stay here. Charles and I can do what is necessary for Richard.'

She nodded. 'Thank you, Silas. If I cannot be by Richard's side myself then I am content that you should be here in my stead.'

'Will you take some refreshment before you leave, Allegra?'

'I am not hungry, thank you, Charles. I would prefer to return as soon as possible.'

'No, Allegra, you must eat before you leave. And I believe there are other guests here; it would be rude to leave so abruptly, would it not?' Tremayne said softly.

She smiled, finding she had no energy to argue. 'I had forgotten about Emily and Edward being here. Charles, are you and Arabella joining us as well?'

'I shall endeavour to locate my wife. If you go to the small drawing-room we shall be there presently.'

Allegra attempted to follow him from the room but Tremayne refused to release her. 'My love, we need to talk before you go. Will you walk in the garden with me?'

He guided her to the French window and expertly released the two catches. It was pleasantly warm on the terrace, but thankfully shaded from the heat of the sun. They strolled in companionable silence, a new experience for both of them. He was the first to speak.

'Allegra, I shall be blunt, you know I cannot tolerate deceit or prevarication. Have you had a change of heart? Am I wrong in thinking that you no longer find this union of ours repugnant?'

She refused to face him, finding his penetrating gaze unnerving. 'Yes, you are correct. I am now reconciled to our match.' Her heart pounded uncomfortably but he did not react as she expected.

'I'm relieved to hear that, my dear. I understand how hard this has been for you. But I promise I'll not make any demands on you after we are married, if that is what you wish.'

She did not answer. She could not. He mistook her silence for lack of comprehension. She heard him clear his throat before continuing.

'What I mean is, we can remain married in name only, if that is what you want. I shall not come to your bed unless you ask me to.'

Allegra felt her face suffuse with colour,

this was plain speaking indeed! He was waiting for her response. Hastily she nodded, indicating that she understood, but remained mute. For the moment she could not find the words to tell him that she was most eagerly anticipating sharing her bed, and body, with him.

She now knew that she was not a cold woman like her mother had been, one who wished to shun all physical intimacy. She realized that the reason she had never been able to respond to her many admirers was because her feelings had not been engaged. The instant she recognized her love for Silas she had felt herself thawing, from the inside out. She had finally solved a conundrum that she had never understood.

She was a woman who reacted only to a man she had feelings for. But all her reticence, her strict upbringing, made it impossible for her to tell him what was in her heart. She prayed that when the time came her actions would show that she wished to be a real wife, to experience everything he had to offer. Her lips bowed and she felt a second surge of heat as she imagined just how much her future husband might have to share. This gave her the courage she needed to speak.

She knew he was waiting, assessing every nuance of her behaviour. Slowly she faced him, eyes wide, her mouth smiling. 'Silas, I am innocent but not ignorant. I know what will be expected of me when we are wed and I am content with that.' She saw his eyes darken and his neck, revealed by his lack of a neck-cloth, convulsed. 'I have behaved badly, and for that I beg your pardon. You have done nothing to deserve my enmity — you are a true gentleman. It is I who have behaved like a person of no breeding.'

He reacted as if she had slapped him. His face hardened and he viewed her with a look of icy contempt. 'I see that I have been deluding myself. You will never change. In your eyes I shall always be your inferior; you will always despise me.' He loomed over her and she could not prevent herself recoiling. 'I'm glad that you understand what your *duties* will be, my lady. These *duties* are the only reason that I wish to marry you. If I could offer you a *carte-blanche*, then believe me I would do so.'

'You are despicable. How could I have considered otherwise?' Her heart in pieces, but her back, as always, straight, she fled, hurriedly retracing her steps to the small drawing-room. Outside she paused, her breathing ragged, trying to regain control before entering.

The sound of feet pushed her into action

and she almost fell into the room in her anxiety not to renew the conversation with a man who was buying her favours — who thought of her as no more than Haymarket ware. He was prepared to put a ring on her finger first, but the intention was still the same.

Edward Grierson, now grown into his looks, jumped to her aid. 'Allegra, what is wrong? I hope the news is not worse than expected?'

'No, thank you, Edward; Richard has lost the sight of his right eye, which is tragic, but no more than I anticipated. I am afraid I clumsily tripped on my hem.' She paused, was Silas going to follow her in? His heavy footsteps could be heard receding and she released her breath.

Allegra accepted Edward's arm and walked over to greet Emily. She noticed the abundance of food laid out on the side tables. 'Emily, I see our luncheon is here. Shall we make a start? Mr Tremayne will not be joining us and I believe that Miss Tremayne and Miss Murrell have had trays sent up to them.'

Emily rose gracefully from the padded settle, the ribbons and bows that decorated her primrose-yellow walking dress swirling round her matching slippers.

'Good heavens, Emily! Were you intending to tramp around the fair in those? You would ruin them in five minutes,' Allegra could not prevent herself exclaiming.

'I have half-boots here; I sent them to the boot-room. But they do not look well with my gown. I intended to change before we ventured out. I suppose we will not be visiting the fair now.'

She embraced Allegra fondly, as though they were bosom bows. 'Do you admire my new bonnet? I adore it, but I am finding the plethora of fruit is making me quite dizzy. For every time I move my head it jounces and bounces in front of my eyes.'

Allegra was forced to smile. 'Then I should remove it, Emily; I intend to remove mine. We are friends, and as your father, Lord Grierson, frequently says, we do not stand on ceremony here.'

'I shall do so. But, pray excuse me, whilst I run upstairs to find someone to assist me.' She watched in horror as Allegra prepared to untie the silk ribbon that secured her bonnet. 'Surely you do not intend to do so in here, in a drawing-room?'

'Indeed I do, Emily. But please do not let my doing so prevent you from seeking assistance. Perhaps you can discover Charles and Arabella and bring them back with you.'

She had heard that the younger girl had recently become engaged to a thrusting young major, temporarily stationed at the barracks in Colchester whilst he trained up a troop of reserves to transport back to the Peninsula.

'I had forgotten how pretty Emily is.' She paused before continuing, 'But rather young for her years.'

Edward, who had watched his sister dash out, shrugged his shoulders philosophically. 'She is a sweet girl, the best sister any fellow could have, but I am forced to admit that she is not exactly a blue-stocking.'

Allegra was forced to smile at his remark. 'And you, Edward, you have changed so much in the three years since I last saw you. I do believe you are now considerably taller than me.'

Edward sauntered over to stand beside her. He topped her by half a head. 'I have grown and filled out. I am taller than Charles.' He picked up a plate. 'Allow me to serve you some of this delicious array. Heaven knows how long Em will be.'

She viewed the plates of elegantly arranged cold cuts, salmon in aspic, meat pasties, pickles, chutney and cheese. 'I wish I had more appetite to do this justice. But I will have a small portion of the salmon and some tomatoes and a sweet roll, thank you, Edward.' Allegra left him at the buffet and sat at the octagonal marquetry table that had been laid ready for them.

Edward handed her a half-filled plate. 'Are you certain that is enough? There is food here to feed an army.'

'Then you had better consume three plates yourself, Edward, or their cook might be offended.'

It did not take long for Allegra to eat her fill. She wiped her lips and drank a little from a glass of freshly made lemonade. Edward pushed back his chair and returned to the table to pile his plate for a second time.

'There are dainties here, and pineapple slices, shall I fetch you some?'

'No, thank you, I have had sufficient. But please carry on — I love to see a man with a healthy appetite.' Chuckling he returned to the table. 'Tell me, Edward, what are you planning to do with the rest of your life? You must be eighteen now, time enough to have made a decision.'

'Did you not hear? I have my colours. Theo, the Earl of Wister, Marianne's husband, purchased them for me, for my name-day gift.'

'A soldier? How exciting! Which regiment do you join?'

'I am to go with Major Denning, Emily's betrothed. I begin my training in Colchester on Monday.' The door opened and their hosts, with Emily, came in. Edward scrambled to his feet. 'We have started. I hope you do not mind?'

'Not at all, as long as there is plenty left for us,' Charles replied. He surveyed the plates with satisfaction. 'I have not broken my fast yet and I am famished.'

The two girls did not wait to be served by either gentleman but piled their own plates, chattering non-stop, completely ignoring Allegra, and choosing to sit at the second table on the far side of the room.

Charles, smiling fondly at his wife of scarcely two months, came to sit with Allegra and Edward. 'I apologize for both my wife and sister, Allegra. They are desperate to spend as much time as possible together. When Emily marries next month she is travelling with the major. The girls have never been separated since they were in leading strings. It will be hard for Arabella to lose her closest friend.' His eyes were weary and he appeared far older than his age of three and twenty.

Allegra hated to see him so low. Impulsively she patted the clenched fist resting next to his plate. 'I am to be married in August as well and shall continue to live at the Priory. I would be delighted to become a closer friend to Arabella if she wishes it.'

'Thank you, Allegra. It is a kind thought, but I rather think Arabella would be happier spending time with Miss Demelza. They are closer in age and temperament.' He grinned at her. 'Do not poker up, you know what I mean. I love my Bella, I would gladly die for her, but I am not blind to her faults. I promise you she would drive you to distraction in a very short space of time.'

Allegra relaxed again, and returned his smile, but inside she was hurt. Was she so austere, so judgemental, that Charles did not consider her as a suitable companion for his young wife?

'Richard and Miss Demelza are supposed to marry in August also but I expect, in the circumstances, the ceremony might well be postponed. He will not wish to stand up at the altar until he is fully recovered.'

Edward dropped his cutlery loudly on his empty plate. 'That was an excellent repast. If you want to know what I think, it is that Miss Tremayne is far too young to be getting married. She is scarcely out of the school-room. It would be better for her to have a season before settling down to matrimony.'

'You are quite right, Edward. But their

affections are engaged and they are determined to wed at the same time that Mr
Tremayne and I exchange our vows.'

Edward stood up. 'That is the same as Em.
There was no persuading her to wait either.'
He half-bowed. 'Please excuse me, I have
promised to meet up with some cronies. They
will be waiting for me at the Plough.' Without
waiting for an answer, or bidding the young
ladies goodbye, he left the room, closing the
door behind him.

Charles frowned. 'I apologize for my
brother. He is not usually so uncivil.'

Allegra's shoulders moved in a delicate
shrug. 'It is no matter. It has been a morning
fraught with difficulties. Which reminds me
Charles, as we are being outspoken, I wish to
know why Richard was obliged to climb that
tree? Why was a gardener's boy not sent
instead?'

'There was no one else. When I decided to
give all the staff the day off, I had no idea that
stupid animal was going to become stuck in a
tree. By the time I required someone they had
all departed. As far as I was concerned it
could have stayed up there. But Bella was
weeping and crying and would not come in to
dress. So when Richard and Miss Demelza
arrived and he offered to fetch it down, I
could see no reason to refuse.'

The haunted expression had returned and Allegra wished she had not asked. 'Of course that is how it was. I should not have mentioned it. Richard has climbed so many trees without mishap, why should anyone have expected it to have been different today?'

She stood up. 'Charles, could you find someone to fetch Miss Tremayne and Miss Murrell down? Also could you ask the stables to send round our carriage? I have no wish to attend the fair today and shall return to the Priory as soon as I have seen how Richard is.'

He bowed. 'Bella, my dear, Lady Allegra is leaving and you have not exchanged more than a few words with her.'

★ ★ ★

The carriage rattled homewards, its occupants quiet, lost in their own thoughts. Allegra kept reliving the conversation with her fiancé which condemned her to a loveless marriage. It would seem that she had found her love for him but lost, irretrievably, any hope of him reciprocating her feelings.

Why her chance remark should have so mortally offended him she was at a loss to understand. She had said far worse before and he had shrugged it off. Why, this time,

182

had he reacted so violently? Still, she supposed, it was better to know how he felt, than discover it too late.

She dipped her head, hiding her wet eyes under the brim of her bonnet. She had been told often enough, by her nanny, her governess, and her mother, that a lady in her position must never show any emotion. That at all times one must remain composed and in control.

But for some reason, today she could not keep her shell intact. If this was what being in love meant, she wanted none of it. She hated feeling so overwrought, so emotional. She clenched her mittened hands and came to a decision. She would eradicate her love for Silas Tremayne from her heart. He did not deserve it so she would destroy it, starting that very second.

However her eyes continued to fill and when Miss Murrell pressed a large cotton square into her hand she took it gratefully.

12

Demelza, sitting diagonally to Allegra, was unaware that her future mama was in distress and blithely addressed her. Richard's accident had not, it seemed, had a similar effect on her composure.

'Lady Allegra, why did Richard not let us in to see him?'

Quickly Miss Murrell answered. 'My dear, he would not wish to upset you. When he returns tomorrow he will be glad of your company. He has never been one to enjoy being an invalid.'

This appeared to satisfy Demelza and the barouche lapsed once more into quiet. Allegra sensed that they were travelling on Witherton land and her spirits revived a little. Surreptitiously she dried her face and pushed the handkerchief into her reticule.

'Miss Murrell, the staff will not know about the accident. Could I ask you to inform them?'

'I shall do so gladly, my dear.' Lord Witherton and Mr Tremayne will require some necessities. Do you wish me to organize their valets to convey them to Great Bentley Hall?'

'Yes, if you would.' Her voice was listless and even Demelza noticed something was amiss.

'Lady Allegra, are you unwell? Do you have the headache?'

Again Miss Murrell stepped in. 'She does, Miss Demelza, so it is best we do not disturb her with idle chatter.'

'I have megrims sometimes. I have to stay in bed and — '

'Yes, yes, my dear, but hush now. We are almost home. You run along to your rooms, I have duties to perform but will be with you shortly.'

On hearing that hated word Allegra's tears flowed anew. Her companion spoke quietly to her.

'I suggest that you remain here, my dear, until you are feeling better. I shall have Abbot come down to attend you.'

Allegra nodded, unable to speak. She felt the carriage rock to a standstill, heard the other occupants descend, but her head remained bowed. How long she sat, alone, she had no idea. She was aware of a movement beside her.

'My lady, come along. Let me help you to your bedchamber.'

Gratefully Allegra grasped Abbot's arm and with her help completed the manoeuvre to the ground. With her dresser's arm around her waist she stumbled inside. The distance from the blue corridor, up the stairs and along the blue gallery, had never felt so far. It was a supreme effort of will for her to keep upright. Eventually she felt the softness of carpet beneath her boots and knew she was almost there.

'In you come, my lady. Jenny and I will help you disrobe. You sit still; we can manage without any assistance from you.'

Like a doll they raised her arms, lifted and lowered her, until the cool slither of her nightgown settled around her naked form.

'There now, lie back and sleep, my lady. You will feel much better in the morning.'

Abbot's voice was the last thing she remembered before slipping into the first, dreamless and refreshing sleep she had experienced since her father's suicide.

★　★　★

The sound of her bed hangings being pulled back and the appetizing smell of chocolate dragged her from her slumber the next morning. For a moment she remained, eyes closed, revelling in the almost forgotten sensation of waking rested. She could hear birds singing, the distant sound of voices coming through the open windows.

She sat up, eyes clear, ready to face the day. 'Good morning, Abbot. Are there rolls and strawberry preserve on my tray? I find that I am hungry this morning.'

'There are not, my lady, but Jenny can go directly to fetch some for you.' The tray was placed on a bedside table. 'Shall I pour your chocolate?'

Steaming cup cradled in her hands Allegra settled back in her cocoon of well-plumped pillows. She sipped the strong dark drink with appreciation. Had her appetite returned as well? Jenny appeared with a plate wrapped in a clean damask cloth. The aroma of freshly baked bread wafted around the room. 'Put them on the tray, Jenny. I shall help myself presently.'

She sipped a little more of her drink before returning the cup to the tray. The rolls had been split and strawberry jam melted from the centres. Eagerly she selected one and raised it to her mouth, The conserve oozed red and thick from the warm roll and, as she watched, the red became blood dripping from lacerated flesh.

With a scream she flung it from her and her stomach convulsed ejecting the hot chocolate she had consumed so happily minutes before. In the aftermath of the nausea the full horror of the day's events flooded back. Richard's injury, Tremayne's brutal words and her decision to stop loving him.

It took the combined efforts of Abbot and Miss Murrell to calm her sufficiently to administer a large dose of laudanum. When drugged oblivion began to sweep her away into the darkness she went willingly, glad she could escape the misery that she felt, not just for Richard but for herself.

She did not stir for the rest of that day and when she showed little sign of recovering by the evening both Abbot and Miss Murrell became concerned. Thomas was sent to ask Mr Tremayne to return; both ladies felt that as her fiancé he was the person to deal with the crisis.

★ ★ ★

Doctor Jones pronounced himself satisfied with Richard's progress. 'My lord, you have no fever. It will be in order for you to return to St Osyth tomorrow morning, but you must rest for another three days, to allow the wounds to heal.'

'That will be no hardship. I have no intention of appearing in public until I look a little more presentable.'

'Excellent, my lord. Light meals only, and no alcohol.' This last remark he addressed to the manservant standing attentively beside the bed.

'I understand, sir. Word will be sent ahead to Cook.'

Doctor Jones bowed and left the patient in the efficient hands of his valet. Tremayne was in the sitting-room, his face serious. 'How is he? When can he be moved?'

'He is making good progress and can be moved tomorrow morning, when it is not so warm. I shall call in to visit him the next day, but do not hesitate to send for me if you feel any anxiety before that.'

Tremayne, immaculate in dark-green top-coat, calfskin inexpressibles and his usual intricately tied neck-cloth, showed no visible signs of strain. He strode into the sick-room. 'Well, Witherton, you can return home tomorrow morning. Your face is not looking so bad this evening — in a few days you'll be able to properly assess the damage.'

'I am in no hurry to view myself in a glass, I can assure you, sir. But until I do, I have no wish for Demelza or Allegra to visit me. I hope they understand this.'

'They do. In fact they returned to the Priory immediately after your accident in order to give you the privacy you requested.'

The tap on the door interrupted their conversation. James, Richard's valet, answered the summons. 'There's a messenger from the Priory, sir. It seems it is urgent.'

Tremayne's eyes narrowed, but otherwise he remained unmoved. 'I shall be there directly. Have him wait in the hall for me.'

Richard waved him away. 'Go, I am well served here. Charles can deal with anything my man cannot manage.'

'If you are sure, lad, I shall go and attend to this latest drama.' He smiled. 'Have no doubt it is of no more importance than that Demelza wishes to quiz me on your condition.'

Once outside the bedchamber his demeanour changed and he covered the distance to the hall in seconds. Thomas stood, hat in hand, awaiting his arrival. 'Well, Thomas, what is it?'

'It's Lady Allegra, sir. She is taken poorly. Miss Murrell wishes you to return immediately.'

The words had hardly left the coachman's mouth before Tremayne was out of the front door, taking the steps in one leap and speeding towards the stables. 'Fetch my saddle. I shall get Apollo,' he shouted to Thomas, who pounded along at his shoulder.

Both men were mounted and away in less than five minutes from the delivery of the message. They galloped across country, jumping the walls and hedges, their horses devouring the miles. When they arrived at the Priory, Tremayne threw the reins to Thomas, vaulted from his saddle and raced inside, his stomach roiling and his face pale.

He arrived, his appearance dishevelled, his boots dusty, it was a little over an hour since the summons had been sent. His knock brought Miss Murrell to the door, her expression anxious.

'Oh, Mr Tremayne, I am so glad you are here. Lady Allegra was unwell this morning and I was obliged to give her a dose of laudanum to settle her. But she has not come round. She is still asleep. Nothing we can do will rouse her.'

'How much did she swallow, for God's sake?'

'A teaspoon — no more — that is why I am so concerned. It cannot be the poppy juice that keeps her comatose.'

Tremayne wanted to rush into her bedchamber but restrained his impulse. He needed to know more. 'You said she was unwell earlier today, in what way?'

Miss Murrell described what had happened and he frowned. 'Did Lady Allegra bang her head on anything? Could she have had a fall during the night?'

'No, sir. She slept well. In fact, it was the best night's sleep she has had for years. Abbot told me so.'

'Why have you not sent for Dr Jones? Why did you send for me instead?'

Miss Murrell flushed and hesitated. 'Her ladyship was most distressed in the carriage on her return yesterday. I have known her all her life and have never seen her weep before, not even when she was whipped for disobedience by her mother.'

'God in His Heaven! What have I done? This is all my fault.' Ignoring her protests he pushed his way into Allegra's room. It was dark, the shutters closed, the bed curtains remained open.

Allegra lay like an effigy on her bed. With a gasp of despair he flung himself across the room, snatching her up in his arms. He rocked her gently, as he crooned her name. Was he too late, had his anger caused her death?

★   ★   ★

Her dark world was moving; Allegra felt as if she was afloat on a choppy sea. Someone dear to her was calling her name, begging her to return from her journey, to open her eyes. It was Silas. He was here, holding her close to his heart, whispering sweet nonsense into her ears. When her eyes flickered open she saw him transformed. The intimidating stranger was gone and in his place was a man, his cheeks unashamedly wet, his eyes gazing down at her with love.

'My darling, thank God, thank God. For a moment I thought I had lost you. That somehow you had taken an overdose of laudanum.'

'Silas? Is that you? What are you doing here?' He had been forced to place his ear close to her mouth to hear her words.

'I came because you are ill, my sweet. Your ladies sent for me.' He punctuated his words with kisses, dropped, featherlight across her face until his lips found hers and stilled. Her mouth opened and she drew in his taste, his smell, his love. He made no attempt to deepen the kiss, content to move his mouth softly across hers, murmuring endearments and apologies until her head was spinning.

With a feeble hand she pushed him away. 'Enough, Silas, you are overwhelming me.' Instantly contrite he prepared to vacate his position on the bed. 'No, stay here, I am still a trifle heavy-headed. Just hold me, my love, let me feel your arms around me, let me know that I am safe.'

Ignoring the scandalized expressions of both Miss Murrell and Abbot, he leant forward and heaved off first one boot and then the other. His jacket followed, then his stock. He grinned at Allegra and her lips curved in an affectionate smile.

Then he was back beside her, his dark head resting on her pillow, and his long legs stretched out on the cover. 'Sit forward, sweetheart,' he instructed. She did so willingly. 'There, lean back; rest your head on my shoulder and sleep. I have you safe in my arms.'

She settled back with a deep sigh of contentment. Over the past thirty-six hours she had been somersaulted from happiness to despair and back again. She was emotionally exhausted. When she was more rested, she would ask Silas to explain what had happened, but for the moment all she needed to know was that he was here, holding her close and that he loved her. The rest could wait.

★ ★ ★

Tremayne gestured to the shocked watchers that they should leave and with bad grace they retired, leaving him alone on the huge tester bed with Allegra cradled his arms. He smiled as the door was left ajar behind them. She was his now. Spending the night together, however innocently, meant that she would be obliged to marry him or her good name would be destroyed, her place in society gone for ever.

He heard her breathing become soft and slow and knew she was asleep. He relaxed, prepared to stay awake all night guarding his prize. But his triumph began to sour. Could he be content for her to marry him, never knowing if she did so from choice or because she was obliged to? Gently he extracted his arm and slid across the bed. His stockinged feet made no sound on the boards. Quickly he collected his scattered belongings and crept out.

'Thank the Lord for that,' Abbot exclaimed under her breath. 'Is Lady Allegra asleep, sir?'

He smiled, glad his beloved had such devoted staff. 'She is, Abbot. I shall sleep in here, if you have no objection, and you can sleep in the bedchamber with her ladyship.'

'That I will, Mr Tremayne. I promise if she stirs I will call you instantly.'

'Good. Ring for a tray to be sent up. I have not eaten since I broke my fast this morning.'

★ ★ ★

When Allegra woke it was barely dawn. The birds' early-morning chorus filled the room with magic. It matched her mood. She was not perturbed by Tremayne's absence as she had woken in the night to seek the commode and Abbot had explained. How thoughtful; how could she ever have imagined him to be less than a true gentleman?

She swung her legs over the edge, making sure she did not disturb Abbot, quietly snoring on a cot at the foot of the bed. Her silk wrapper was draped, as usual, over a chair back and she slipped it on. She crept across the chamber and pushed open the door, catching her breath in delight when she saw her beloved Silas sprawled, more off than on the chintz-covered *chaise-longue* he had selected for his bed.

Asleep he looked so much younger, the lines around his mouth and eyes smoothed out, his fine dark hair flopping endearingly over his eyes. She barely resisted the urge to run across and fling herself into his arms. If he could be strong, do the right thing, then so could she. She was beginning to move backwards when he spoke, his eyes still closed.

'Darling girl, are you well? Do stop dithering in the doorway in your undergarments. Go away at once. For I swear, if I open

196

my eyes and see you *en déshabillé*, I shall not be responsible for my actions.'

With a gasp, half of pleasure, half of fear, she skipped back inside the safety of the chamber, closing the door firmly behind her. The noise awoke her guardian.

'My lady, you must not go out dressed as you are.'

'I shall not, Abbot. I was at the open door a second or two, no longer, and Mr Tremayne was still asleep. I needed to know he was outside.'

Abbot shook out her crumpled gown; she had not undressed for her night vigil. 'If you'll excuse me, my lady, I will retire to my room and make myself more presentable. Shall I rouse the kitchen for your chocolate?'

'No, it is far too early. I shall sit by the window and listen to the birds singing and watch the sun come up across the park. There is no need to hurry, I am quite content.'

By the time the Priory was awake Allegra was bathed and dressed in her favourite morning gown: a simple blue and white sprigged muslin, with a sash and petticoat that exactly matched her eyes. Her sitting-room was restored and her lover gone. But his message, written on her own stationery, had been explicit.

My darling Allegra
I implore you to meet me at eight o'clock
in the library. Do not be late
.   *Silas Tremayne*

★   ★   ★

Her lips curved every time she read it. Even his note was a mixture of endearment and direction. Richard was returning later, at ten o'clock, but before that she had her assignation. The hands of the ormolu mantel clock refused to move this morning. Five minutes seemed like fifty.

'It is time, at last. I am going down, Abbot. I shall be back to change, I intend to ride out to meet the carriage bringing Lord Witherton home.'

On light feet she flew downstairs, her radiance, her glow of happiness, sending more than one young male servant reeling. The library door was open and she rushed in. Her smile faltered.

'Silas, what is wrong, why do you look so fierce? Is Richard worse?'

He ignored her flustered questions and asked one of his own. 'Do you know what these are?' He held out two rolls of parchment neatly tied with red ribbons. The agreements she and Richard had been obliged to sign.

'Yes, I do.'

'And these, can you guess what these might be?' He gestured to a box filled with flimsy scraps of paper and other official-looking items. She peered at the box.

'My father's vowels? Mortgage documents perhaps?'

'They are. Sit down on that chair by the fireplace.'

Intrigued, she sat and waited, she could do nothing else. Her gaze drifted to the empty grate and she realized it held kindling. She watched him gather up the papers and tip them on top of the sticks. He knelt by the chimney breast and picking up the tinderbox, he struck it against the kindling making several strikes before the sparks caught fire.

She held her breath as the papers that tied her to Silas crumbled into ashes. He was setting both Richard and herself free. Giving them back their inheritance. He loved her so much he was letting her go. How could he? She did not want to be free — she wanted to be tied to him for life. Was he so blind he failed to understand how much she had changed towards him?

Tremayne watched the papers disintegrate, reduce to grey dust, before he moved. Then, still on his knees, he moved to face Allegra. He lifted his head and gazed into her heart.

'My love, will you do me the honour of becoming my wife? No, think about it, do not answer too quickly. You have your inheritance restored; you can marry anyone you want.'

'Silas, you are a nincompoop! The only man I want is you — I love you. If I cannot have you, I shall have no one.'

His gamble had paid off. With a roar of delight he regained his feet and lifted her from the chair. When he set her down again they were both breathless.

'You do comprehend, Silas, my love, that you are now my guest and I can have you evicted if I so desire?'

'You can try, sweetheart, but I would not lay wagers on your success.'

Giggling she pretended to push him but her attempt ended with a squeal as he tossed her into the air and, tucking her under one arm like a parcel, headed for the door. Squirming with embarrassment she was carried through the corridors to the breakfast parlour, leaving a series of servants open-mouthed with astonishment.

'That was uncalled for, Silas. You are far larger than I; you used brute strength to prove a point. If you had used your intellect I should have been more impressed.' Rigid with annoyance she stepped up to the sideboard, groaning under the weight of silver epergnes containing food. She stared at them; for the first time in her life aware just how extravagant her lifestyle was.

'There are thirteen of these here and just four of us to eat the contents. Silas, what have I been thinking of? What a terrible waste, when so many country folk are going hungry.'

Unmoved by her sudden conversion to philanthropy he began removing the covers. 'Would you like ham, coddled eggs, scrambled eggs, buttered mushrooms, porridge . . . '

'Stop this at once, Silas. This is no laughing matter.'

'Sweetheart, what do you think happens to the leftover food after every meal?'

'I had not considered.' Her brow furrowed. 'I suppose the staff finish it.'

'Of course they do. Why do think they are all so healthy and well fed? If you cut the amount your cook prepares, your staff will fare less well each day.'

'I am not convinced that it would not be better to allow extra funds for their rations and have the food prepared especially for them.'

'Good God! I am marrying a radical! I had no idea you harboured such revolutionary ideas, my love. Next you will propose we pay pensions to our staff and keep them free of charge until they die.'

She was unsure if he was teasing. Then she remembered his threat to turn the Priory old folk off. 'You are a scoundrel, Silas Tremayne. You have no right to poke fun at me.'

They passed away the time happily bickering and enjoying every moment of it. It was a novelty for both, to have someone they could laugh and talk with and not need to worry about causing offence.

'I am going to ride out and meet Richard; will you come with me, Silas?'

His face sobered. 'You cannot, my dear. He asked expressly for me to keep both you and Demelza away until he is more recovered. I believe he is worried about your reaction to his injuries.'

'He is worrying unnecessarily on my account. And I cannot imagine for one minute that Demelza will be repulsed, not if she truly loves him.'

Tremayne was not so optimistic. He knew that the initial attraction for his daughter had been Witherton's good looks. 'I sincerely hope you are right, Allegra. Your brother truly loves her and he has lost so much already.'

'He has his inheritance back. Maybe that will be enough for him.'

'Would it be for you?'

Allegra felt as if she had swallowed a stone. Richard and she were twins. If he had given his heart, then like her, nothing else would make him happy. No amount of wealth could ever compensate for losing that love.

13

A closed carriage brought Lord Witherton home at the expected time to what must have seemed like a ghost house. Not a soul visible inside or out, apart from Tremayne, who was waiting by the door to welcome him.

'Witherton, allow me to offer my arm, you still look a trifle unsteady.'

'Thank you, sir; I can manage with the assistance of my man.' He negotiated the entrance, but was forced to pause to recover his strength before attempting the stairs. 'I am confoundedly weak still. It is only my eye I have lost, not a limb, I cannot understand it.'

'You lost a lot of blood, lad; such a serious injury sends the body into shock. You'll be back to normal in a day or two, I guarantee it.'

Richard's shoulders slumped. 'No, sir, I shall not. My face is ruined. I shall never be the same.'

'When the swelling and superficial cuts heal you will see that the damage is not so dire. Doctor Jones suggests you wear a patch; have you considered doing so?'

'A patch?' Richard half smiled. 'I could start a new fashion — patches were all the rage not so long ago, although smaller and worn on the cheeks — but it is an idea. Thank you, sir.' He progressed slowly up the first few stairs, leaning heavily on the arm of his valet. 'How is Demelza taking this? And Allegra?'

Tremayne joined him. 'Allegra is desperate to see you; she has news for you. Do not shut her out, Witherton. You must know that her sensibilities are not so fine that she will be upset by the consequences of your accident.' The fact that he didn't include Demelza in his speech did not escape Richard.

'As soon as I am comfortable, I shall send for her, sir.'

Tremayne watched his future brother-in-law complete his laboured ascent before returning to the morning-room, where Allegra waited impatiently for news. She greeted his appearance with a smile.

'Well, Silas, how is he? Can I go up and see him?'

'Yes, my love, you can. He intends to send word as soon as he is settled.'

'I cannot wait to give him the good news. Did he mention Demelza? Ask to see her as well?'

Tremayne shook his head. 'He asked how

she was, but did not ask to see her. I think he is preparing himself for the worst.'

'Will Demelza cry off? Break the betrothal?'

'It is a distinct possibility, I fear. But I shall not interfere. You're not the only one who has changed, my darling.'

He held out his hand and she took it. Together they strolled out into the garden redolent with the sweet scent of honeysuckle and summer jasmine. They settled on a stone bench, warm from the sun.

'Tell me, Silas, in what way have you changed?' She saw his cheeks colour and for a moment he looked like a penitent schoolboy.

'I decided, when I was refused entry to the homes of the *haut ton*, that if I could not walk freely in the highest establishments then my grandchildren would certainly do so.' She nodded, smiling to encourage him to continue. 'I began my search for a suitable match for Demelza three years ago. I noticed your brother then; he was too young, of course, but so was Demelza. But he had everything I wanted. Excellent breeding, intelligent, and neither a hard drinker nor a gambler. And he was the handsomest man on the marriage market.'

'I can hardly credit that you have been planning this for so long. That you knew about Richard, about me, before I knew of your existence.'

He ignored her interruption. 'Your brother was perfect. But he had no reason, at that time, to wish to tie himself to the daughter of a cit.' He gave her a quizzical look. She flushed at this reminder of her earlier incivility.

'So when my father appeared and started gambling away our home and wealth, you stepped in?'

'Exactly. I can assure you that I did not instigate his ruin; he did that all by himself. I merely bought up his scripts, made sure it was my banker who offered him mortgages when he ran out of funds.'

'And when did I feature in your schemes?'

His arms tightened round her waist and with his free hand he tilted her face. 'When I saw you on the morning that I first arrived here.'

He swallowed her startled exclamation with a swift kiss. When he lifted his head she was in no doubt what had prompted his sudden decision to make her his bride.

'I can hardly believe that you had that document drawn up so quickly. I would not have thought a man with your reputation could be so impulsive.'

He chuckled. 'When I see something I

want, sweetheart, I take it. And I wanted you.'

She stiffened in his embrace, remembering his cruel words on this very subject.

'My darling, I will apologize again for my cruelty when we were at Great Bentley Hall. I'll admit that it was desire prompted me at first, but that soon changed, almost immediately, to love.'

'And I continued to treat you so callously. I too must beg your pardon; I deeply regret my behaviour.' She rubbed her face against his shoulder. 'I am sorry to tell you, my love, that I only recognized my love for you two days ago. It is strange how blind I was to my feelings.'

'Have you ever fancied yourself in love before?'

Startled, she sat up. 'No, of course not! How can you suggest such a thing?'

'If you had, you would have acknowledged the emotion sooner. Anyway, I don't give a damn when you discovered it, as long as you are certain of your feelings now.'

'Of course I am. But, Silas, my dear, please refrain from using such bad language. My ears are permanently burning from your profanities.'

In answer he scooped her on to his lap. 'I shall endeavour not to swear, if you promise to kiss me whenever I want you to.'

It was there, embracing, that James, Richard's valet, discovered them. He coughed and stamped noisily on his approach giving them time to separate. 'Lord Witherton would like to see you now, my lady, if that is convenient.'

She scrambled to her feet. 'I shall come at once.' She forgot to bid Silas goodbye in her eagerness to see her brother.

★ ★ ★

Richard's room was darkened, the shutters and curtains drawn. For a moment she could not see him in the gloom. 'Please do not hide from me in the darkness. I love you; you are my twin.'

Reluctantly he moved towards her and she ran forward into his fond embrace. She stepped away and, still gripping his hand pulled back the curtain. In the dappled sunlight that filtered through the shutters she examined him.

'You are no longer the most handsome man in the country, but even with one eye you will still be devastating.'

'I am disfigured, Allegra, do not pretend it is otherwise.'

'But I have come to tell you that you have regained your birthright.' She explained all that had taken place in the library that morning. When she had concluded her tale he was dumbstruck.

'I can hardly believe what I have heard. My home, my wealth restored? I no longer need to marry to maintain the Priory?'

She nodded; pleased her news had animated him. 'Does this news make a difference to your relationship with Demelza?'

He threw back the shutters with a bang. 'It does indeed. If I am not obliged to marry then I do not have to hide away, in case I scare her off. She can see me, make up her own mind. I will not hold her to her promise. If she wishes to break the engagement so be it.'

'You would give her up so easily? I thought you loved her.'

His smile was sad. 'I do, that is why I must let her go if that is what she wants. Take her to London, there must still be a few soirées and musicals to attend. Give her a brief taste of society. When you are her mama you can give her a proper season. Obtain vouchers for Almack's, maybe present her?'

Allegra was quiet for a moment. 'I shall do as you suggest, Richard. Take Demelza to Town. I would also like to introduce Silas to my friends and acquaintances. They will not dare refuse him entrée now.'

'Then the matter is settled. Shall I send for Demelza, speak to her as well?'

'I suggest that you leave it until we return. Let her have a brief taste of Town life. Either she will come back determined that she is in love with you, or ask to break the connection. Then you will know it was not your injury that sent her away, but that her affections were not truly engaged.' She hugged him a second time. 'Go to bed, Richard, you look fagged to death. I shall speak to Silas and then make the necessary arrangements to open Witherton House.'

★ ★ ★

Before dawn, two days later, Abbott, Tremayne's man, Sam Perkins, and Demelza's maid set off. It had been agreed that both their town houses were to be opened. As Tremayne's establishment was also in Brook Street they deemed it more appropriate if he resided there.

At a little before nine o'clock the travelling carriage, the height of modernity and with every imaginable luxury, waited outside. Three pairs of matched blacks stood champing at their bits. Thomas was driving; John, an under-groom, an expert with a blunderbuss, was to sit beside him. Two further grooms were travelling on the rear step, cudgels tied securely to their waists. Tremayne had his pistols primed and ready, tucked into the pockets in the door of the coach. He had no intention of taking chances with his precious cargo.

'We are to break our journey at Chelmsford, at the Saracen's Head. I have bespoke rooms for us. The baggage cart will meet up with us there,' Tremayne told the ladies as they trundled down the drive.

'Shall we get to London by tomorrow night, Papa?'

'I sincerely hope so. However, in order to do so, we must depart before seven o'clock. Do you think you can be ready by then?'

Demelza grinned. 'I can rise early if I wish to. I am so looking forward to visiting Town. In my last letter from Lucy she told me that she was intending to visit at the end of May, so she should be in London already. Her parents have taken rooms at an hotel, Grillons, I think it is called.'

'They are just making a short visit?'

'Yes, Lady Allegra, Lucy wants to see the Tower and the menagerie, and go to watch the fireworks at Vauxhall Gardens and to the theatre to see a play by Will Shakespeare — '

Her father halted her in mid-sentence. 'Then we must ensure that you and Miss

Carstairs meet and then you can make your visits together.'

Delighted with his suggestion Demelza turned her attention to Miss Murrell, sitting opposite, and they deliberated at length on such important matters as gowns and fal-lals. Allegra smiled at her intended. He responded by stretching out his booted feet catching her own within them. They had no need to chatter of inconsequential things, they were content to sit in silence. Eventually even Demelza ran out of words and, like a small child, curled up her feet and prepared to place her head in her father's lap.

Allegra hurriedly leant forward and untied the ribbon that secured Demelza's bonnet to her head. 'There, you will be far more comfortable now, my dear.'

'Thank you, Mama.'

A quiet giggle followed this remark and her father stroked his daughter's glossy black hair. He glanced up at Allegra and his loving smile sent waves of heat coursing round her body. She had made the right choice. He was the one man who could make her happy.

She relaxed into the well upholstered squabs and her eyelids drooped. It was more than three years since she had paraded in the salons of the *haut ton*. She was known as being very high in the instep, a real stickler for protocol. How would these acquaintances react to her betrothal to exactly the sort of man she had so recently despised? Silas wanted to be part of all walks of society, not just accepted by the gentleman in their clubs but by the ladies in their drawing-rooms. She frowned as she considered how best to tackle this problem.

'What is it, sweetheart? Is something worrying you?'

Her eyes flickered open and she saw the concern etched on his dear face. 'Nothing, my love; at least nothing that need bother you. I was considering which invitations to accept, indeed who might still be holding parties so late in the season.'

★　★　★

The night spent in Chelmsford passed pleasantly enough. The rooms, although a trifle cramped, were well kept and the bed linen crisp and clean. Their early start was not to Demelza's liking and she promptly fell asleep again immediately the carriage was on the move. Very soon all four occupants were dozing, all bareheaded, their hats neatly stowed under the seats in the compartments provided for that purpose.

It was a warm day and even stopping twice

for refreshments failed to relieve the tedium of the journey. Tremayne spoke to Thomas before they resumed.

'We are somewhat later than I had hoped to be, Thomas. This means we shall be obliged to cross the heath and run through Feathers Wood at dusk. Those places are notorious for footpads and highwayman. Have your weapons prepared, make sure they are loaded and give two to the boys on the step.'

'Yes, sir. We will keep our eyes peeled. If we are accosted, what do you want me to do, whip them up or brazen it out?'

'Use your initiative, Thomas. Do what feels safest. But I am certain all this preparation is unnecessary, we shall, like the majority of travellers, reach our destination unscathed. The landlord told me the local militia flushed out all the riffraff last week; there have been no attacks since then.'

'But you are right to be alert, sir, that way we all know what to do.'

Allegra poked her head from the open window curious to know what the delay was. 'It is so hot in here, Silas; we are in the sun. If you are going to be much longer can the carriage be moved into the shade until we are ready to depart?'

'I am coming now.' He jumped in, his

weight rocking the carriage dramatically and causing Demelza to lose her balance.

'Papa, you're not suited for a carriage. You're far too large,' she admonished him, giggling as she pushed herself upright again.

'Believe me, I should much prefer to be riding Apollo, but I could not allow you three delightful ladies to travel unaccompanied, could I?'

'Fustian! It is too far to ride and you know it,' Allegra told him laughing. 'Although, if you had travelled post, you would be in town by now.'

He grinned, arranging himself more comfortably in the corner. 'I could, my love, but I would be considerably the poorer for the privilege. Travelling post is exorbitantly expensive.'

Allegra arched her eyebrows a fraction and he chuckled. 'I know; I am as rich as Croesus but miserly in my spending.'

'I do hope not, sir, for I intend to be an extravagant wife. I shall demand a new gown for every day of the week.' Still laughing the party settled into their respective places.

'When do you think we will be there, Papa?'

'Another few hours, I'm afraid. But the sun will set soon and then it will be more comfortable in here.'

The carriage continued at a leisurely pace, the horses were not as fresh as they had been the day before. By using three pairs the load was less but even such fit and healthy beasts as these began to tire after forty miles of pulling a full carriage under a hot sun.

As the interior of the coach cooled Allegra noticed that Silas had become more alert. She watched his eyes stray several times to the pockets in the carriage door.

'Silas, what is in the door that interests you? Are you secreting jewellery of great value?'

He shook his head and raising his finger to his lips. She knew he did not want her to wake Demelza or Miss Murrell. She leant forward to hear his answer.

'There are pistols in the door; I do not like travelling this stretch when it's getting dark, so it's best to be prepared,' he whispered.

Allegra nodded and reached into the leather pouch beside her and drew out the gun. She was an excellent shot and familiar with this type of firearm. 'I shall put it here, in the pocket inside my skirt. If we were accosted, a bandit would not expect me to be armed.'

He did not argue, but followed her lead and removed the second loaded gun tucking it into his belt. 'You're a constant surprise to me, my love. I am learning new things about you every day.'

'My father taught Richard and me together.' She patted her travelling bag. 'I have something similar in here. Remember, I am well used to travelling this route.'

The coach gently swayed to a stop. Thomas called down. 'I am just lighting the lanterns, sir, nothing to worry about.'

This gave Silas the opportunity to change position. He indicated to Allegra that she should shuffle along the seat and then he took her place by the window. She could feel the pressure of his thigh against hers, the thickness of his buckskin unmentionables, and the folds of her French green cambric travelling dress not sufficient to prevent his body heat sending a frisson of excitement round her already overheated body. She was glad that in the darkness of the interior her wanton behaviour could not be observed.

Lanterns lit, the coach resumed its journey. The coachman urged the horses into a spanking trot. Tremayne was not alone in his dislike of travelling this particular patch as night approached.

His arm left the safety of his lap and travelled around her waist, pulling her even closer. She dared not look up, expose her mouth to his; what they were doing was quite risqué enough. She felt his fingers sliding upwards until he cupped her breast. Her head fell sideways, on to his chest, and heat pooled in a most unexpected region.

Then his weight shifted violently and she cried out as she was flung to the floor. The carriage rocked and she could hear Thomas fighting to control the horses. From her position crouching by the door she watched Silas, pistol in hand, disappear into the darkness. She could hear Miss Murrell comforting Demelza.

'Get on to the floor, away from the open window. Quickly, do it now,' she ordered. It was best not to take chances. She heard them slide down beside her in the well between the seats. She knew what was happening: they were being held up. Cautiously she peered through the slit of the door, expecting to see a row of footpads or at least a highwayman on his horse, brandishing pistols, and demanding their valuables.

It was not so dark that she could not see that the road ahead held nothing more alarming than a fallen tree. The grooms from the rear step were frantically trying to drag it aside. There was no sign of Silas anywhere.

She sat up, quickly hiding her pistol. 'The road is blocked; I am going to see if I can help. It is safe to resume your seats.'

It was a long way from the carriage to the road without the steps and she decided to slide out feet first. She dropped her legs over the edge and was carefully feeling for the ground when Silas spoke quietly from somewhere behind her.

'For God's sake, stay inside, it's an ambush, I'm sure of it.'

She froze. Her stomach lurched and for a second she was unable to think clearly. It was no wonder the grooms were working so hard — at any moment they expected to be mowed down by an unseen attacker lurking in the darkness of the woods.

Then she moved, not back into the comparative safety of the carriage, but out into the danger. If Silas was out there, risking his life for them, then she would be with him.

Keeping the door half closed she slithered through the gap and dropped silently to the ground. She rolled under the carriage, between the wheels, from there she could see but remain invisible. Slowly her eyes adjusted to the twilight and she stared around. She could still see the grooms working to remove the tree but where was Silas hiding?

There was little room to manoeuvre under the carriage and she was obliged to shuffle painfully until she could see the far side of the road. It appeared to be deserted. Then she glimpsed, or thought she did, a movement in the undergrowth.

Yes, she was certain, there were men hidden beneath the overhanging branches. She swallowed the bile that rose in her throat. This was not an ambush by common thieves; this was something far more sinister.

How could she warn Silas without revealing her position? She scrabbled about in the dust with one hand until she found a stone. She slid her arm round, hitting her knuckles painfully on something protruding from the wheels, and hurled the missile into the bushes where she had seen the movement.

The result was even more successful than she could have hoped. The stone found a soft target and the man discharged his gun in surprise. The bullet tore harmlessly into the canopy of leaves but the return fire was instant and deadly. The scream of agony from the trees meant at least one man was wounded. Then she saw a pair of boots she recognized as belonging to Silas.

She could not hear any orders but she saw the two grooms dive behind the protection of the fallen tree trunk and then their guns fired into the trees as well. Another howl of pain and then there was the sound of running feet fading into the distance.

It was over. The ambush had been routed. They were all safe. She felt movement from above and then heard Miss Murrell talking urgently to Demelza. She began to inch her way backwards, as there was more room to move down the centre of the carriage.

Silas called to his men, 'Go and see what we hit, but be careful, load your guns first.'

Demelza, frantic with worry for both her father and Allegra, threw back the door and jumped out.

'Get inside, now, sweetheart.'

His warning came too late as a single shot came from the bushes on the side nearest the carriage. Without a sound Demelza crumpled to the ground.

14

Everyone froze — suspended in disbelief. Then several things happened at once. Silas dropped down at his daughter's side. The two grooms paused, and then continued their cautious approach to collect the wounded men from the far side of the road.

Thomas jumped down to offer his assistance, but Allegra's eyes were fixed on the place in the bushes from where the flash of the gunshot had come. No one else was looking that way, all, in those first few seconds, concerned with the fallen girl.

She backed out of her hidey-hole, her pistol cocked and ready. She could see someone studying the scenario, believing he was safe, ignored by those who were armed and dangerous. He did not appreciate his position. She raised her arm and steadied her breathing. With deadly accuracy she fired and the hidden man reared up clutching his chest and toppled sideways, dead.

Silas jumped up, cracking his head on the swinging carriage door and swore loudly. 'Thomas, who fired that shot, for Christ's sake?'

'I did,' Allegra told him quietly as she emerged from behind the carriage, her smoking pistol dangling at her side. 'I was under the carriage and saw it all. He was watching, gloating; I could not allow that.' The voice was even, her words clear, but her eyes were empty.

'Miss Murrell, come out here. Take care of Demelza. She is winged, not badly hurt, thank God.'

Silas grabbed the older lady's arms swinging her down to the ground. Stepping round his daughter, he removed the gun from Allegra's icy hand, pulling her into the warmth of his embrace.

'Darling girl, it is over; you did well. I'm proud of you. That vermin deserved to die.' He felt her struggle in his arms, her attempts became more frantic.

'Silas, I am going to be sick.'

He stepped aside, not a moment too soon as, with a horrible retching, she cast up her accounts. He held her until the heaving was over. She leant weakly against the carriage, grateful for the steadying arms around her waist. Her skin was clammy and her hands were shaking too much to wipe her face. Gently he removed his handkerchief from his jacket and completed the job for her.

'I apologize; that was most unladylike of me.'

'Indeed it was, my love. Whatever will you do to shock us next?' Tremayne, moving his feet carefully to avoid the noxious mess, lifted her back into the carriage. 'Sit quietly inside, sweetheart, whilst I deal with Demelza's injury.'

She needed no further urging. She felt faint, her head still spinning unpleasantly. Slumping back against the seat she thanked God that the outcome had been no worse, that Demelza was not badly hurt.

In that split-second, when she had seen Demelza's body on the dirt beside her and thought her dead, she had never felt such rage, such anger. She believed that she now understood what Captain Pledger had once spoken of, that soldiers felt a 'killing rage' and in this state could hack and dismember their enemies without conscious thought. At the time she had considered this description a little far-fetched, but now she realized it was true. This was not the time to dwell on what she had done.

Outside she could hear Miss Murrell tearing strips from her voluminous cotton petticoat to make bandages. Thomas was talking quietly to Silas, but she was unable to catch his words. She was temporarily removed from reality, drifting in a state somewhere between consciousness and sleep, and she could not bring herself to take any further part in the proceedings. Demelza was not badly hurt and Silas was well, what more did she need to concern herself with?

Thomas had finally let down the steps and Miss Murrell climbed back inside. Then Silas entered, Demelza in his arms, and carefully placed her on the seat, her head in Miss Murrell's ample lap.

'There, darling, rest, you're going to be fine. You feel unwell because of the shock; your injury is not deep, hardly more than scratch.'

Demelza recovered enough to answer. 'That's all very well for you to say, Papa, but it is not your shoulder that is hurt.'

'I know; I am an unfeeling brute. I have been told so many times before.' He smiled down at his daughter. 'I think you are more concerned about missing out on parties and excursions than your injury.'

She returned his smile. 'It will take more than this to stop me. I have been anticipating this trip to Town for ever. Lucy and I talked of little else when we were at that horrible seminary you incarcerated me in for so many years.'

He backed out of the carriage, brushing his lips across Allegra's forehead as he passed. 'I must stay behind, to clear up, my love. I am keeping John with me, Thomas, Billy and Fred can see you safely to the next hostelry.'

'Be careful, Silas. Keep your pistols loaded,' Allegra roused herself enough to whisper.

'I shall, my dear. Thomas has instructions to send back assistance as soon as you arrive at your destination.'

★　★　★

The carriage moved off, harness creaking, its lanterns bobbing in the gloom, leaving Tremayne with a single lantern and a single groom, to seek for corpses. This was no accident; it had been meticulously planned, but why anyone should wish to murder a member of his family, he could not hazard a guess.

He went first to the spot from which the near fatal shot had been fired. 'Hold the lantern up, John, whilst I poke around in here.' He parted the branches and immediately found what he sought. The light waved wildly for a moment and then was steady again.

Face down he saw the body of a man dressed in what, at first glance, appeared to be verminous clothes, exactly what one would expect from such a villain. Then he beckoned the lantern closer and with his boot he rolled the corpse over on to its back.

The muffler the man had used to obscure his face had slipped and now hung limply round his neck. What was this? The man was all but clean-shaven, and had, as far as he could see, undamaged teeth. No footpad he had ever come across had such a face as this; broken teeth, lank hair full of creepers, that was more usual.

He crouched beside the body, holding out his hand for the lantern. He placed it by the man's outstretched arm. Gripping the cuff, he carefully raised the hand until it was within the yellow pool of light. The watching groom cried out in shock.

'My gawd, sir, this is a toff! He ain't no regular footpad. He has fingernails and smooth hands.'

Tremayne dropped the hand, his suspicions confirmed. He shone the lantern directly over the pallid face but he was certain the man was unknown to him. Why should a stranger wish to harm him? No, confound it! It was not him the man had been after. He had been in his sights for some time, an easy target. It was only when he had called out to Demelza that the shot had been fired.

His scowled in concentration; had he used her name? He had not. He had called her sweetheart. In the dark could the murdering bastard have thought he was talking to his fiancée, to Allegra? Was she the intended target? After all they were of similar build, and dressed alike, and in the dark the difference in their colouring would not have been obvious. But he dismissed the idea immediately; the assassins must have been after someone else. It had just been a near tragic mistake.

His smile was grim. Well, at least one of them had paid the ultimate penalty. None of it made any sense. He had made enemies, of course he had, but had not made his fortune out of another's ruin. All had been won fairly, through hard work and an acute business sense. He did not know the answers now but, by God, he intended to find out.

He grabbed the lantern and strode off leaving the body, eyes open, staring into oblivion, to search the far side of the road. At least two of their attackers had been hit, but whether fatally he had yet to discover.

The trampled undergrowth was easy to spot, even in the darkness. He had had his fill of corpse hunting. He needed to think. 'You take a look in there, lad. See if there are any more bodies.'

The young man dived into the undergrowth and was soon crashing around, the lantern swaying crazily. 'Nothing here, Mr Tremayne, but lots of gore. They must have got away whilst we dealt with Miss Tremayne.'

'It's as I thought, you can come back now. I don't suppose you have a tinderbox about your person?

'No, sir; but there's one in the coach.'

'I expect there is,' Tremayne replied drily. 'Gather up any loose branches, dry grass, twigs; anything that will burn. We must make a fire by the side of the road. It is quite possible that a coach could still come by and we want to be seen.'

Carefully Tremayne ignited a sliver of dry wood from the candle inside the lantern and transferred the flame to the waiting fire. At his third attempt, the air blue with curses, he finally succeeded and the pile of wood blazed brightly. He extinguished the candle and settled down for a long, boring wait.

★　★　★

In a little over an hour, Thomas expertly turned the carriage into the flare-lit yard of a busy coaching house. Allegra had recovered from her dizziness and was ready to do what was necessary. She smoothed back Demelza's hair. 'We have arrived, my dear. You will have to stay here with Miss Murrell whilst I go and arrange matters. I promise it will not be long before you are tucked up snugly in bed.'

'Will my papa be here soon? Will Richard be coming as well?' The injured girl had already asked this question several times.

'Yes, as soon as we send back for him. Not long now.' Allegra was deeply concerned. Her patient's condition had deteriorated on the journey. The sooner that she got Demelza inside and fetched a physician to attend her the better.

Miss Murrell assisted her with her bonnet whilst she replaced her gloves. The steps were lowered and she descended, well aware that her crumpled, dusty dress contrasted badly with her silk-lined, pristine chip straw bonnet.

But whatever her appearance, no one doubted her pedigree. Accompanied by Thomas, who had handed the ribbons to Billy, she stalked into the vestibule. Fortunately there was only one person waiting to be dealt with. The other travellers, from the mail coach standing in the yard, were on their way to the dining-room for supper. As they had but thirty minutes to consume it and reboard the vehicle, they had no time to stare.

The stout country gentleman, waiting at the counter, stepped aside to allow Allegra to approach. She was relieved to find the landlady in attendance.

'I have a seriously injured lady in my carriage. We were set upon by footpads in Feathers Wood. She has been shot in the shoulder and requires the attention of a physician immediately. I need two rooms, each with private parlour, is that possible?'

'Oh, my lady, what a dreadful thing! Upon my word I thought those wretches had been dealt with.' She rang the brass bell by her side loudly and two girls appeared, who from their matching appearance, were obviously her daughters. 'Annie, send Jack at once to fetch Dr Canning; tell him a young lady has been shot in the shoulder. Beth, run to the kitchen and have them prepare clean linen strips and boiled water for the doctor's use when he arrives.'

Mrs Foster, the landlady, curtsied to Allegra. 'I will direct you to your rooms myself.'

Allegra led the way back to the carriage. Two ostlers held the horses' heads and Fred and Billy, the second coachman, were waiting by the open door. 'Thomas, will you carry Miss Tremayne upstairs? She is too unwell to walk.'

He ducked into the interior emerged backwards, his feet guided by Fred and Billy, Demelza in his arms. Miss Murrell followed, hastily securing her own bonnet.

'This way, my lady,' Mrs Foster said, 'please to follow me.'

The rooms they had been allocated were at the front, overlooking the yard. The largest had an adjoining sitting-room; the second was adjacent, but not connected. The rooms were clean and well kept but not ideal.

'I am sorry, but are there any rooms in a quieter location? I believe Miss Tremayne will not do well with so much noise outside.'

The landlady thought for a moment. 'I have a small room and parlour at the rear, overlooking the garden, but only the one.'

'Excellent. Please direct us there. Miss Murrell and Miss Tremayne can have those rooms. I shall take these. My fiancé, Mr Tremayne, will be arriving later and will require a room. The smaller chamber will be adequate for his needs.'

Demelza was quickly settled, her outer garments removed, her chemise serving as a nightgown. Allegra drew Miss Murrell to one side and addressed her softly.

'I have to leave you for a while. I must send word to Brook Street for they will be expecting us tonight. I must also ask Abbot and Sam Perkins to return to us.'

'I can manage here, my lady. I shall sponge Miss Demelza to keep down her fever — but I hope the doctor comes soon. I fear her injury might be worse than we had at first thought.'

Thomas was standing in the narrow passageway waiting for her. 'Have you arranged for the horses and acquired some accommodation for yourselves?' Allegra asked him.

He nodded. 'Billy is seeing to that, my lady. Mr Tremayne told me to stay with you. I've also got Fred searching for a cart to drive back to collect Mr Tremayne and John.'

'Thank you.' They came to the second passageway. 'I have no idea in which direction my rooms are. I was not paying attention.'

'If you allow me, my lady, I can conduct you.' Thomas stepped past her. 'This place is old, more like a warren than a dwelling.'

The rooms were found and Allegra was pleased to see a tray with a tureen of steaming broth, fresh bread and cheese and several slices of apple pie, standing on the sideboard in her parlour.

'If you would wait. I shall write my letters, then you can arrange for them to be sent.' She scanned the room but even in the light of a dozen candles she could not see a writing desk. 'Botheration! There is no stationery here. I shall have to send down for some.'

'I will fetch what you need, my lady. It will save time.'

The door closed behind him leaving Allegra alone. The appetizing aroma from the soup sent her into the bedchamber in search of water to wash. She was surprised how heavy the jug of water was to pour out and how difficult to keep it in the bowl.

As she washed she glanced round the room — the beamed ceiling was low, and she doubted Silas could stand upright without hitting his head. But, like the other rooms, it was immaculate and the bedlinen smelled of lavender.

Pleased she could sleep without fear of being eaten alive, she dried her hands and neatly folded the cotton square she had used. Now she felt ready to tackle the supper tray deciding that she would eat before writing her notes.

She was spooning up the last of the savoury soup when Thomas returned with her writing materials. 'The horses are stabled, my lady, and there is a fine supper waiting in the snug downstairs. I told Billy to eat before he leaves.'

'Good — and you have beds for the night, I hope?'

'We do, a back room behind the stables, and we don't have to share with anyone else either.'

'You have been a great help, Thomas. Go

and have your meal; it will take me a while to compose these letters.'

Allegra trimmed the quill and uncorked the lumpy ink. They were not what she was used to but would serve her purpose. She penned a note to Abbot, asking her to return with Perkins and bring sufficient clothing for all of them for a short stay. She instructed them to travel by post; that way they could be at the hostelry where they were staying by morning.

Next she wrote to Richard; after all he was still Demelza's fiancé. He was fully recovered from his accident and quite able to travel to London if he wished to do so. But whether he was ready to expose his face to the gaze of the public was another matter.

She folded the letters, melting a blob of wax to seal them, then pressing her crested ring into each. They needed to be sent on their way directly. She had heard the mail coach depart noisily a few moments ago so knew the inn would be less busy.

She decided not to wait for Thomas to return to collect the letters. She would take them downstairs herself. It would only take a minute or two to speak to Mrs Foster, ask her to find two members of her staff who were willing to undertake the arduous journey.

Finding her way back to the entrance hall was simple, all she had to do was follow the din coming from the bar. With her candlestick held aloft, and her skirt lifted high in the other hand, she descended the winding wooden stairs.

The landlady greeted her appearance with dismay. 'My lady, you should not have ventured down here alone. We have a party of gentlemen recently returned from a cock-fight and I'm sorry to say that they are a trifle disguised.'

So the raucous laughter that had directed her to the vestibule came from them. 'I shall be quick. I would like these letters delivered. This one, to Brook Street, is urgent, and I should like someone to deliver it immediately. They can travel post. The other is not quite so urgent. I have the requisite coins here to pay for both.

'My lady, I do not have two lads to spare. Can you not send one of your grooms with the second?'

'Very well, have your man go to Brook Street; I shall organize the other.' Allegra dropped some coins in to Mrs Foster's outstretched hand and turned, intending to retreat before she could be accosted.

She was too late. 'Good heavens, Lady Allegra, what are you doing in this benighted place?'

'Captain Pledger! What a surprise.' She was

aware of the anxiety of the landlady, hovering behind her. 'It is all right, Mrs Foster, I am well acquainted with this gentleman; he is a close friend of my brother, Lord Witherton.'

'We cannot converse here, my lady. It is too public.' Captain Pledger turned to Mrs Foster. 'Do you have a private parlour we could use for a moment?'

'No, sir, we don't, we are that full tonight, they are all in use.'

'Captain Pledger, I have a parlour, come upstairs with me, for there are things I must tell you.'

Ignoring the scandalized snort from Mrs Foster she led the way back upstairs. She must put her enmity aside. Captain Pledger's arrival at the White Hart was a godsend. He could take the letter to Richard and accompany him back. The captain was a soldier; he would be ideal to watch over him. Although she cordially disliked him, he was a friend of her brother's after all.

She led the way back upstairs to her sitting-room. She did not notice him pull the door shut behind him. 'I must begin by apologizing for my treatment of you when we last met, Captain Pledger.'

He bowed, his expression hidden from her. 'It is already forgiven and forgotten, my lady. I fear that something is amiss. How can I be of assistance?'

Hurriedly she related the events of the past few days. He was suitably appalled by it all.

'I shall be delighted to take the note to Richard, Lady Allegra. I am quite prepared to ride all night.'

'Thank you for the offer, but the matter is not that urgent. If you take the next mail coach — I believe that they leave from here twice a day — that will get you there soon enough.'

'I would prefer to ride. I have my horse with me; he has been resting for several hours and is fit enough to take me half the distance. I can hire a nag for the second half of the journey and collect my mount on the return.'

'If you are going to leave at once, you will, no doubt, see Mr Tremayne waiting by the side of the road. Would you be so kind as to tell him that we have arrived safely, that Billy is on his way, and that we are awaiting the arrival of a doctor for Miss Tremayne?' Allegra hesitated. Should she offer to fund his journey, or would he be offended.

'I shall be glad to leave my friends in the bar. We won a small fortune between us, and they are determined to drink their share away.'

'Then I shall thank you again, Captain Pledger, and look to see you in Brook Street with Richard in due course.'

He bowed again and it was then she realized the parlour door was shut. She felt herself flushing, how could he have been so foolish? It was far too late to point out his lack of thought, any damage to her reputation was done.

She peered up and down the passageway and was relieved to discover it was empty. She had been closeted with him for scarcely ten minutes, even if during that time the matter had been noticed it was hardly long enough to constitute a serious breach of etiquette.

It was high time she returned to see how Demelza did. As far as she was aware the doctor had not arrived. Unwilling to risk further indiscretion she went to the bell-cord and pulled it vigorously. This time she would get a maidservant to escort her.

Allegra took turns with Miss Murrell to cool Demelza's burning face. 'It is more than an hour since we arrived; why has the doctor not attended us?'

'I am sure he will be here soon, my lady.' No sooner had she spoken than they both heard the sound of voices and footsteps approaching down the uncarpeted passageway. 'This could be him coming this very minute. I shall let him in at once.'

Doctor Canning examined his patient. 'It is

a flesh wound, but it is deep and requires a suture or two.'

Miss Murrell acted as his assistant and the job was completed efficiently. Demelza hardly stirred even when the doctor cleansed the injury with brandy.

'Why is she so hot, Doctor Canning? I thought fever did not set in until the next day.'

He completed his ablutions before replying. 'My lady, Miss Tremayne lost a lot of blood, and the long carriage ride did not improve matters. However, I do not believe her life to be in any danger at the moment. Keep sponging her down, keep her cool, and get as much boiled water down her as you are able.'

'Thank you, Doctor Canning. Do you have any idea how long we shall be obliged to remain here?'

'It depends how Miss Tremayne is in the morning. But even if her fever abates, I doubt that she will be well enough to travel for a day or two.'

The maidservant, who had waited outside, came in to remove the soiled cloths and water. 'Will you be requiring anything else, my lady?'

Allegra shook her head. 'No, that will be all, thank you.' She turned to Miss Murrell.

'Have you had any supper?'

'No, my dear. I should have asked the girl to bring me up a tray. But I suspect the kitchen will be closed now, for it is past nine o'clock.'

'There is a tray in my room. The broth will be cold, but there is bread and cheese and apple pie. You go and eat; I will take care of Demelza in your absence.'

As the door closed softly behind her companion Allegra belatedly realized she had neglected to tell her about the meeting with Captain Pledger. She would tell her when she returned. She rubbed her eyes — she was so tired — it had been a long and difficult day. Perhaps if she splashed her face with cold water before returning to her vigil by the bed she would feel more able to cope.

15

The fire flickered and snapped loudly making John jerk. 'Steady, lad, it's a twig. There's no one but ourselves out here now.'

The groom grinned. 'Sorry, sir. I'm a mite jumpy. It's not every day you get to share a fire with a corpse.'

Tremayne folded his legs under him and stood up, walking to the centre of the lane. 'Listen, can you hear anything?'

'I do, sir. I reckon a carriage is coming. We will see the lights as soon as it rounds the bend.'

'Hand me my jacket, John. I need to tidy myself up or the driver will think we are the bandits.' His cravat, long past recovery, had been discarded earlier, but served as a polishing cloth for his boots. 'I need a shave, but it's so dark I must hope no one will notice.'

'Shall I light our lantern, now, sir?'

Tremayne nodded. 'Yes, stand in the centre of the road and swing it slowly, give them warning of our presence.'

They stood, side-by-side, John holding up the lantern as the smart equipage drew nearer. It halted within hailing distance, but out of range.

'I am Silas Tremayne. This is my groom. We were set upon earlier and have remained behind guarding the remains of one of the attackers.' His words carried clearly to the stationary vehicle. His explanation was accepted and the carriage rolled forward, the four horses pulling it snorting and stamping at the delay.

Tremayne remained where he was, giving the occupants of the coach time to study him more clearly, be sure he was a gentleman; that this was not a clever ploy to ambush them.

The groom on the box jumped down and ran round to open the door and lower the steps. Tremayne watched, hoping there were no ladies present. A tall man, of middle years, his evening coat straining across his chest, descended and strode confidently towards him.

'Sir Bertram Davies, at your service; this is a bad business, sir. I hoped I had cleared the buggers from these parts last week.' He pumped Tremayne's outstretched hand. 'Show me that cadaver, Mr Tremayne, let me see if I recognize him.'

In the light of four lanterns Sir Bertram stared down at the corpse. 'It is no regular footpad, sir.'

'I had come to that conclusion myself. I fear the ambush was premeditated. When my daughter was shot it was a deliberate act. It was not me they were after, but either Demelza, or my fiancée, Lady Allegra Humphry.'

Sir Bertram nudged the corpse with his boot. 'Well, we will discover nothing new out here, it is far too dark.' He shouted over his shoulder. 'Bring a blanket from inside the coach; we have a body to wrap up.'

Ten minutes later they were ready to depart. John was travelling on the step at the rear with strict instructions to look out for the cart coming out to fetch them. Inside, the blanket-shrouded shape lolled in one corner, Tremayne and Sir Bertram, sitting on the opposite side, ignoring their macabre companion.

'I am the magistrate in this region. It was my militia flushed out the vermin last week. We have five fine specimens waiting for the gallows.' The older man was all but invisible in the darkness. 'However I can assure you none of them looked like that one over there.'

'In the hour or so I have been sitting by the roadside I have considered every possible reason there could be for someone wishing to kill a member of my family and am no nearer a solution.'

Sir Bertram delved in his jacket pocket and pulled out a silvery flask and offered it to Tremayne. 'Here, sir, you must be in need of some refreshment. It is French cognac — although I should not own to having it, I suppose.'

Tremayne swallowed several mouthfuls of the fiery liquor. 'Thank you. That is exactly what I needed. Of course, a simpler explanation could be that it was a case of mistaken identity. We were stopped in error, and in the darkness the attackers took us for someone else.'

'I have a third suggestion for you, Mr Tremayne. A possible answer to this conundrum. But it is possible you might not like my idea.'

'I wish to hear it, nevertheless, Sir Bertram.'

'In my experience when a female is targeted, there is a jealous lover involved in the perfidy somewhere.'

Tremayne's jaw hardened. He drew breath to deliver a pithy response but something held it back. He knew that Allegra had no lovers, jealous or otherwise, but he had. Camille had not taken her dismissal kindly and had, according to his messenger, made wild threats, had threatened to get her revenge. At the time he had dismissed the tale as of no importance, but had he been wrong to do so?

'I think it is just possible you might be correct, sir. There is someone in my past who made threats when I ended the liaison. I shall investigate the matter further when I return to Town.'

'Good man! That's the ticket. Then I shall leave the matter in your hands. What do you wish me to do with the body?'

'Nothing. I shall take it with me, if you have no objection. I wish to examine it more carefully in daylight. There might be something secreted in a pocket somewhere.'

'No, take it, sir;' send the cadaver on to me when you have finished with it.'

The sound of a horse galloping towards them interrupted their conversation. From the open window Tremayne caught a glimpse of a man, crouched over the withers of a powerful horse, and then he was gone, the hoofbeats fading into the night.

'Good God! He was in a deal of a hurry,' Sir Bertram exclaimed. 'He will break his neck if he takes the next stretch at that speed; it is full of potholes.'

A while later John called from his vantage point behind the coach, 'I can see lights approaching, Mr Tremayne. I reckon it's Billy with the cart.'

The moonlight illuminated the road ahead now it was no longer obscured by the dense thickets of Feathers Wood. The carriage rattled to stop and the far door opened. Billy put his head in.

'Mr Tremayne, sir; Lady Allegra is safe at the White Hart, Romford. Do you want John and me to take this with us in the cart?'

'An excellent idea. Are we far from the inn?'

'In this, about fifteen minutes, no longer, sir.'

John and Billy rolled the body through the door and then the steps were folded back and the door slammed shut.

Tremayne broke the silence, a few minutes later. 'Do you have far to travel tonight, Sir Bertram?'

'No, I live a mile away from the White Hart. I shall be snug in my bed shortly after you, sir. I intend to make enquiries locally tomorrow. It is possible the two wounded men were seen by someone. If I discover anything I have your direction and shall send up to you.'

'You have been most kind, sir. I doubt that there are many men prepared to share their carriage with such an object.'

The carriage halted outside the entrance to the yard of the coaching inn and Tremayne jumped out. He was anxious to get inside and see how his ladies did. Sir Bertram had assumed that the dead man had been killed by himself, or one of the grooms, and he had not told him otherwise. The fewer people who knew about Allegra's involvement the better.

Demelza's injury was easy to treat, but the damage to Allegra might be far harder to cure. She had suffered too many shocks recently and he knew, from conversations with Miss Murrell, that her mental state was fragile. Her temporary collapse, only a few days since, had demonstrated that.

He strode into the White Hart to find the vestibule empty. He could hear that there was a drunken party in the public bar and had no intention of investigating there. He rang the bell impatiently. In the quiet his stomach rumbled loudly, reminding him he had not eaten.

The door opened behind the counter and a man appeared, wiping his hands on his leather apron. 'Good evening, sir. Are you by any chance Mr Tremayne?'

'I am. I hope you have a room for me.'

'I do, sir; I have taken the liberty of sending up a tray for you. I expected that you might be sharp set and the kitchen is now closed until the morning.'

'Thank you. I should like to visit my

daughter before I retire. Could you have someone conduct me to her rooms?'

He tapped softly on the outer door a potboy had led him to. Miss Murrell opened it and her face lit up. 'Good evening, sir. I am so glad you have arrived safely.'

'How is Demelza? What did the doctor say?'

'She has a fever, but it is less than it was. Doctor Canning assured us that she is in no danger. Come along through, Mr Tremayne, but I warn you, she is sound asleep.'

Having seen that Demelza was indeed comfortable and well attended, he was eager to find his own chambers. The waiting potboy took him back through the maze of narrow passageways.

'This is yours, sir. You ain't got a parlour, I'm afraid. Her ladyship's next door, but she's retired. There's no light showing beneath her parlour door.'

The boy entered first, holding the candlestick aloft, and from it he lit several candles before departing. Tremayne decided the chamber was adequate; he had slept in far worse over the years. If the supper he saw hiding under a clean white cloth was half as good he would be satisfied.

He tumbled on to his bed fully clothed, too fatigued to remove more than his jacket and boots. He was instantly asleep. He had discovered years ago that however dire the circumstances it was easier to deal with them after a good night's rest.

★   ★   ★

Allegra heard him arrive, his deep baritone was unmistakable and the walls were thin. She had been sitting, in the dark, in her parlour listening out for his footsteps. She wished he had knocked on her door, come to see her, but he must have seen that there was no light and decided it would be indelicate to disturb her once she was in her bedchamber.

No matter, she felt comforted knowing he was so close, within earshot. Now she was ready to retire. She had left the curtains undrawn and the moonlight flooding in through the windows was sufficient to light her to her bed. She removed her grimy travelling dress and tossed it on to the floor in disgust. No amount of sponging would restore it sufficiently to make it wearable. She smiled. If her maid did not arrive by morning, and she was not prepared to remain in her chemise, she would have to put the soiled gown back on.

She said her prayers before slipping between the sweet-smelling sheets. She thought that the Lord must be tired of hearing from her. She seemed to have been in constant communication over the past few days. The banging and clattering in the yard gradually subsided and Allegra fell asleep.

Her dreams were troubled. She was running, trying desperately to find somewhere to hide, but every time she found sanctuary behind a tree the unseen dangers multiplied. Finally she burst into a clearing to be met by a barrage of gunfire.

Men with holes in their chests, with half their faces missing, and with one eye socket gaping bloodily, lurched towards her, smoking guns in their hands. She was surrounded by these monsters. There was no escape. She screamed, again and again.

★   ★   ★

From his bedroom Tremayne heard her screams and, fearing the worst, he grabbed his pistol and hurtled from the room. Her parlour door was locked. Without hesitation he stepped back and raising his foot, prepared to attack the door.

A hand dropped on his shoulder. 'You have no boots on, man. Here, let me do it.' A large young man, cravat dangling round his neck, but fully dressed, smashed the lock with two powerful kicks. Tremayne burst into the room, pistol ready to fire.

Allegra's terrified screaming had roused most of the guests at the front of the inn and several of them prepared to follow, eager to discover why the young lady had been making such a racket. Mrs Foster arrived, her cap askew, in time to prevent them.

'Please return to your rooms, ladies and gentlemen. The young lady's having a nightmare, nothing worse. She was held up on the road today and her young friend was shot. Such an experience must have upset her nerves.'

Nodding and muttering in sympathy, for most had heard about the event, the assembled guests traipsed back to their beds. The screaming stopped, the corridor was quiet again.

In the bedchamber Tremayne was holding Allegra's arms and rocking her back and forth as she sobbed on to his shoulder. 'Darling, it was a bad dream. You're safe, you're safe now. I am here to hold you.'

'Mr Tremayne, shall I take over now? I have dealt with Lady Allegra's nightmares many times before.' Miss Murrell spoke quietly from behind him.

He was reluctant to release her, fearing she was so agitated she might lapse back into the strange semi-comatose state she had suffered from less than a week ago.

But Miss Murrell was insistent. 'It will not do, sir, for you to be in here much longer. Please allow me to take care of Lady Allegra now.'

He stepped back and Allegra's tearstained gaze followed him. 'Do not go, Silas, please stay with me. I had such terrible dreams.'

'I cannot, sweetheart. But I shall stay in the parlour, next door, as I did before. Miss Murrell will take care of you.' He backed out to find both the unknown gentleman and Mrs Foster conversing quietly in the parlour.

'I have sent my girl, Annie, to sit with Miss Tremayne, sir. Your daughter seems much better and she is sleeping comfortably.'

'That's kind of you, Mrs Foster. I'm sorry we have been such a trial to you.'

'That is no matter, sir. It's what we are here for. If you require nothing else, please excuse me. Good night.'

'A good-hearted woman,' the stranger commented. 'She's allowing my friends and me to pass the night here in the bar. We neglected to reserve our accommodation and the place is full.' The man bowed. 'Robert Forsythe, at your service, sir.'

'Silas Tremayne, at yours.' They shook

hands. 'I must thank you for your prompt action. A broken foot would not have helped the situation.'

'I was in the vestibule, trying to persuade the night porter to find me some food. I could not ignore the screams, they were heartrending.'

'Lady Allegra has undergone several unpleasant experiences lately. It is hardly surprising she was overwrought,' Tremayne told him.

'No, indeed. But at least she had one piece of good fortune. A friend of Lord Witherton's, a Captain Pledger, joined our party this evening, and was able to offer her some assistance. That was a fortunate coincidence, was it not?'

'Is he here now, do you know?'

'No, he left a while back. He saw Lady Allegra arrive and excused himself, told us he was an old friend. He did not come back. He had not booked a room either so I have no inkling where he is. Perhaps he has decided to sleep with his mount?'

Tremayne suspected this was not the case. 'I believe he passed us on the road, heading back towards Brentwood. Lady Allegra must have asked him to deliver a message to her brother. My daughter, Demelza, is betrothed to Lord Witherton.'

Robert Forsythe yawned hugely. 'You have the right of it, I'm sure. Now, I will keep you from your bed no longer, Mr Tremayne, and shall bid you goodnight.'

'Forsythe, I'm sleeping in here, on the chair. Although Lady Allegra's companion is sleeping in the chamber with her, I wish to be nearby in case I am needed. So, please take my room. It would be a pity to leave the bed unoccupied.'

Robert bowed again, grinning. 'Presumably you want to collect your jacket and boots before I retire?'

'Good grief, yes!'

★   ★   ★

Allegra heard the voices fade and pushed herself up anxiously. 'He is gone. Miss Murrell I cannot sleep if Mr Tremayne is not outside.'

'Do not fret, my dear, he will be back. I believe I heard him offering the use of his room to the young man who helped him earlier.'

'Please go and see; I do not want to take any poppy juice and shall not dare to close my eyes until I am certain he is there.'

Her companion returned a few moments later. 'Mr Tremayne is back now, he merely went to collect his boots and jacket, that is all.'

Satisfied, Allegra fell back on to the pillows but neither she, nor Silas slept. Miss Murrell, stretched out comfortably on the far side, a bolster pushed between them, snored gently until morning.

Heavy eyed, Allegra slipped out of bed to investigate the sound of a vehicle arriving in the yard below. It was scarcely light, even the cockerels were crowing half-heartedly. A post chaise had just pulled up. A sleepy ostler shambled forward to open the door. To her delight she watched Abbot and Sam Perkins descend. She saw the ostler hurry off to the rear of the building, presumably to fetch help to carry in the baggage.

'Miss Murrell, Abbott and Perkins are here. Will you go down and direct her up to me, please?'

Her companion scrambled off the bed, shaking out her skirts. 'This is excellent news, my dear. They have made good time. We shall all feel a deal better when we have a change of garments.' She hurried from the room, finding Tremayne stretching out his cramps by the door. 'Good morning, sir. Your man is here with your baggage.' She paused. 'Oh dear, you have no room to use. You gave your chamber up.'

He smiled. 'I have things to do outside that do not require clean clothes. Please tell Lady Allegra I shall be back to see her later. Time enough to rouse Mr Forsythe on my return.'

Abbott was greeted with enthusiasm. 'I am so glad you are here for I wish to go outside and cannot do so until I am suitably attired.'

'I'll go down for hot water, my lady. It is early, but the place is stirring. The ostler said the overnight mail coach is due any time soon.'

Allegra hurried to the window. She saw Silas come out and he glanced up and waved, blowing her a daring kiss. She blushed and retreated, belatedly realizing she was still in her chemise.

Breakfast came up on a tray. She knew it would not do for her to venture into the public rooms, already overfull with passengers from the coach. Of her beloved Silas there was no sign. Abbott had visited Demelza and found her awake and devouring a healthy breakfast. What was Silas doing outside for so long? The gentleman, who had occupied his room, had gone downstairs sometime ago.

'My lady, if you put on your bonnet and spencer, I could accompany you downstairs. It would not be unseemly to visit your horses, and see how they are doing.'

The bonnet, in peach silk, stiffened inside by buckram, framed her face to perfection. Her ensemble was, as always, in the first stare of fashion.

Abbott was not happy about her choice. 'That peach skirt will show every mark, my lady. You would have been better in the moss green.'

'I am not changing, Abbott, so it will have to do. Hand me my gloves, if you please. I am impatient to discover for myself what is keeping Mr Tremayne so long from my side.'

The entrance hall was deserted, even the ever-vigilant Mrs Foster absent elsewhere. Allegra hurried through. She was preparing to march round to the stables when she spotted Silas talking to a stranger, a tall young man with an unruly mop of light-brown hair.

'There he is, Abbott.' She viewed the dirt and dung-strewn yard with disfavour. 'I think I shall wait here for him, after all.'

Her abigail, relieved the gown was not to be ruined, decided her serviceable grey cotton and sturdy half boots would take no harm. 'Shall I go over and tell him you are here, my lady?'

'If you would, thank you. I was thinking of waving to attract his attention.'

'No, my lady, you must not.'

Allegra watched her maid pick her way carefully through the mire until she reached the two men, so immersed in their conversation they did not, at first, notice her. Then Silas looked up, and saw her. His face was transformed by his smile. She felt her knees weaken and was forced to grip the door frame for support.

Within seconds he had covered the ground and was beside her. 'My dear, how are you this morning? Did you sleep at all?' He clasped her hands, scrutinizing her face.

'Is that a roundabout way of telling me I look dreadful, Silas?'

'You are enchanting, as always. My love, allow me to present a recently acquired young friend of mine, Robert Forsythe.'

Mr Forsythe bowed deeply and Allegra dipped her head in acknowledgement. 'I am pleased to make your acquaintance, my lady.'

'And I yours, Mr Forsyth. Do you think we had better go inside? We are creating an obstruction and I fear we could be mown down by the passengers returning to their coach.'

Laughing, she led the men upstairs to her parlour. The room which had earlier seemed adequate was now overcrowded. 'There is scarcely room for us to sit in here, but we must make do,' Allegra said, indicating to

Abbott that she should absent herself.

Tremayne propped himself casually on the windowsill, Allegra took an upright, bentwood chair which left Robert Forsythe to perch awkwardly on the one remaining seat, a chintz-covered armchair.

Now, Silas, tell me everything that has transpired since I last saw you.'

For some reason none of them thought it strange that a virtual stranger should be included in the conversation. When he concluded his story she asked eagerly, 'And were there any clues on the body, Silas?'

'Better than that, my dear, Forsythe recognized the man.'

'What? That is extraordinary. Who is he, sir?'

'He was, I am sorry to say, an officer in the Essex Regiment to which I was attached until recently.'

'You are a soldier? I should have guessed it; you have the carriage of a military gentleman.'

'Thank you, my lady. But I was forced to resign my commission — family matters I will not bore you with.'

She waved her hand. 'There is no need to explain; it is none of our business. But please tell me the name of the man?'

'Lieutenant Giles Symons, an impecunious

gentleman, always lived above his means, and was involved in more than one unpleasant incident, to my certain knowledge.'

Allegra hardly dared to ask the question. 'Was he, by any chance, stationed at Colchester or Weeley barracks?'

Forsythe nodded. 'Yes, he was recently at Colchester, involved with recruitment, I believe. Why do you ask?'

Allegra felt her head spinning. If the man was from Colchester, then he might have known Captain Pledger. It was too much of a coincidence to be ignored. White-faced she stared at Tremayne. 'Silas, what have I done? I have sent Pledger to Richard. I cannot bear it; it is too much.'

16

The two gentlemen stared at her with astonishment. Tremayne shook his head. 'My dear girl, what cork-brained notion is this? Pledger is a friend of Witherton's; weren't they at school together?'

Her colour began to return and she thought that maybe she had overreacted. 'Yes, they were. I cannot like him, but I suppose he is Richard's closest friend. I am sorry, I am jumping to conclusions; it was silly of me.'

Forsythe hastened to add his reassurances. 'You must remember, my lady, that Colchester has over six thousand men and Weeley considerably more. Unless Captain Pledger was billeted at one of these barracks, I doubt he would even have met our villain.'

'Richard and Captain Pledger did sometimes frequent the officers' mess in Colchester, but it involved an overnight stay so more often they went to dine in Weeley, which is much nearer to the Priory.'

Tremayne pushed himself away from the window. 'I think I see the doctor on his way up. I wish to speak with him.'

His guest took his cue. 'And I must not detain you. Thank you for your hospitality.' He bowed to Allegra. 'I shall make enquiries at Colchester; the adjutant is a friend of mine and he should be able to ferret out the scoundrel's associates.'

'That is kind of you, sir,' Tremayne said. 'We shall be in Town for the next three weeks; could you send anything you discover to me there? You have the address.'

★　★　★

Doctor Canning pronounced Demelza against all his expectations, fit enough to travel that day. A flurry of activity ensued as bags were packed and arrangements made.

'Silas, do you promise you will be in London in time to take me out this evening?' Allegra asked.

'I shall. I must speak to Sir Bertram, but then I shall, reluctantly, travel post chaise.' He chuckled at her wry expression. 'No expense is too great, my love, when it means I can be at your side more quickly.'

★　★　★

The last stage of the journey was uneventful and the carriage pulled up outside Witherton

House at noon. Thomas handed the reins to Billy and climbed down. In the absence of her father or fiancé he was designated to carry Demelza inside.

'Do you think there is a note from Lucy, Lady Allegra? Could you please find out for me?' Demelza called, as she was being taken up the white marble stairs. Miss Murrell immediately hushed her charge, reminding her of unladylike behaviour. Allegra smiled, how quickly life moved on; a few weeks ago it was she who was being told gently to behave correctly.

There was a neat stack of cards awaiting her attention. The letters she had sent in advance of their visit, informing her acquaintances she was going to be in town, had obviously been received. She flicked through them. Yes, there was a note for Demelza amongst the invitations.

Whilst on her way up to the apartment allocated to Demelza and Miss Murrell, she continued to glance through the cards. Was there one for tonight that she could take Silas to? She was eager to introduce him to society, proud to claim to be his future wife. She smiled as she considered the way her opinions had altered over the weeks. Her society friends would be busily speculating what was the truth behind her betrothal to a man she would have ignored last time she was in Town.

A wave of heat swept through her as she recalled the farewell embrace he had given her. No one who saw them together could doubt her reasons. It was a love match. Their original motivations were irrelevant; neither money nor pedigree came into it at the present. She could hardly wait to see the faces of the town tabbies when she sailed in on the arm of the most attractive, and unlikely, man in England.

Her sudden laugh startled the footman waiting to open the door to the apartment. She was glad to find Demelza reclining on a *chaise-longue*, a patchwork coverlet across her outstretched legs.

'There is a note from your friend, Demelza.' She handed it over. 'And I wish you to call me Allegra; after all we are almost family.'

'Can I not call you Mama?' Demelza asked hopefully.

'I would prefer not. I am only eight years your senior. But I hope to be a loving sister and friend to you instead.'

'I love you already, Allegra. And do you know, I believe that you and Papa will be the perfect match. I have never seen him so happy.' She giggled. 'I believe I've even seen him laugh once or twice as well.'

'Baggage! Have you no respect for your father?' Allegra pulled the covers straight. 'Well, what does your Lucy say? Is she to visit you here, or does she wish you to go to the hotel?'

'She's coming this afternoon to see me. She does not know of my injury; should I put her off?'

'If you stay resting on your day bed, do not move around too much, I see no reason why your friend should not come. But do not make too much of the shooting, Demelza. It will become the talk of the town and it is uncomfortable to be the subject of idle gossip.'

'Shall I tell her we were set upon by thieves and I was shot? I expect it happens to people all the time.'

'I sincerely hope it does not. In fact, you have the distinction of being the only person of my acquaintance who has been so distinguished.'

'Well, apart from military gentlemen. But it is their trade to be shot at, isn't it, Allegra?'

'Indeed it is, my love; also, if Captain Pledger is to be believed, stabbed, slashed and blown to bits.'

Miss Murrell thought this topic of conversation quite unsuitable. 'At what time is Miss Carstairs coming? I think you should have a light repast and a rest before she arrives, Miss Demelza. You do not wish to be too fatigued to enjoy the visit, now do you?'

'No, Miss Murrell,' Demelza chimed obediently.

'Then I shall leave you. I intend to have a sleep as well.' She leaned down to hug Demelza, who whispered in her ear.

'I expect more soldiers die from cholera and dysentery than from battle wounds, don't you?'

'Horrible girl! What a lowering thought! I shall see you later, when we are all rested.'

★ ★ ★

Allegra selected an invitation to an intimate supper and card party to be held by the Dowager Duchess of Avondale, a grand dame with her finger in every society pie. If she approved of Silas, then all the other hostesses would fall into line. She quickly penned a note to be sent round to Silas informing him that he was to present himself at Witherton House, in formal attire, no later than twenty minutes past seven. After leaving instructions for Abbot to wake her at five o'clock, she retired to her chamber.

She hoped she would be able to sleep more

easily when the sun was up, that its brightness would keep her bad dreams at bay. Even after an absence of more than three years the familiarity of her bedchamber was reassuring. She had not slept in this room since her nightmares began and it had no unpleasant associations. She prayed that this would be enough to allow her to rest undisturbed.

⋆   ⋆   ⋆

At seven o'clock Allegra was bathed and dressed in her evening finery, an exotic Indian silk in palest blue with a darker blue gauze overskirt. The cap-sleeves and matching long, silk fingerless gloves were embroidered with tiny blue glass beads in a floral pattern. With her white gold hair piled high on her head, her sapphire and diamond parure, which included ear bobs, a collar and a bracelet, she knew she had never looked better.

'I am going along to see Miss Demelza, Abbot. I shall require you to be in the hall with my cloak and reticule at twenty minutes past seven.' Abbot handed Allegra the ribbon that allowed the demi-train to be held from under her feet and made a few small adjustments.

'That is a beautiful gown, my lady. The colour is unusual but on you it's perfect.'

The footman knocked on the door to Demelza's apartment. A maid opened the door and curtsied.

'Miss Tremayne has retired, my lady, but she is still receiving.'

Allegra's heart sank. It was far too early for a young lady to retire unless she was feeling unwell. 'Demelza, my dear, are you feeling worse? Here, let me feel your forehead.' Allegra was relieved to find the skin cool under her fingertips.

'No, I am a little tired but not poorly.' Demelza grinned. 'I was forced to claim illness in order to escape from Lucy. I had intended to hide in my bedchamber until she left but she insisted on helping me disrobe, so here I am.'

Allegra smoothed out the back of her dress before carefully perching on the end of the bed. 'I take it you did not enjoy your visit? I am sorry to hear that, when you were so looking forward to seeing your friend again.'

'I did not realize how shallow she is. She talked of nothing but clothes, slippers and bonnets until my head was spinning. I find we have little in common now.'

'Perhaps it is because you are feeling rather out of sorts? When you are better you might feel differently about her.'

Demelza's mouth pursed. 'I doubt it! Do

you know I felt more like her elderly aunt than her bosom bow? I believe that I have changed since I met Richard. I see things differently now. Will he be here soon, do you think?'

'I hope so; I sent a note to him telling him of your injury, but he is busy with estate business; he might decide he has not got the time. After all we are only here for three weeks.'

'If he loves me, surely he will come? I would go to him if he had been shot.'

'But you must remember that he is still recovering from his own injuries, my dear.'

'I understand, Allegra. You do not have to cover up for him. He does not wish to marry me now he has had his properties returned. Why should he wish to tie himself to a nobody? He could have anyone he wanted. There are dozens of debutantes more eligible.' Demelza wiped her eyes on the sheet. 'I intend to release him from his offer. I love him too much to hold him against his will.'

'I think you had better wait until you speak to him in person before making such a rash decision. Have you considered he might be feeling exactly the same reservations himself? That you might not wish to tie yourself to a man with only one eye?'

Demelza rocked back, her face pale. 'He could not be so stupid! If he had been blinded then maybe I could understand, but he is my beloved Richard; one eye, one leg or one anything, I shall always love him.'

'In which case, my dear, you have nothing to fret about. Whether Richard comes to London or not, I do not think you have any cause to worry about his constancy.'

'Miss Murrell says I will be well enough to travel back to the Priory in a day or two. If Richard does not come to me I shall go to him. I find the thought of visiting the sights no longer interests me.'

Allegra patted her hands. 'I have to go. Shall I send up your papa when he arrives?'

'No, thank you, I shall see him tomorrow. I suppose Richard will be obliged to stay with Papa, not here, if he does come?'

'I am afraid so, my love. But your town-house is only five minutes from this, hardly a separation at all.' Allegra shook out her dress, hoping she had not creased it by sitting.

'It is fine, Allegra, no lines at all. You will stun my father into silence in that gown; I think you look like a fairy princess out of storybook.'

'And since I met him he has made me feel like one. My feet are floating several inches from the floor most of the time, I am so happy.'

Demelza giggled. 'I seem to recall that you thought you hated my father until quite recently, Allegra.'

'Oh stuff to that! I intend to forget that I was ever at odds with him. I do not wish to ruin my romantic ideal. Goodnight, my love, sleep well.'

★ ★ ★

Downstairs Tremayne prowled, magnificent in his evening clothes, favouring the modern fashion of black pantaloons and slippers, to knee breeches and stockings. Abbot was hovering in the background, Allegra's belongings in her arms. The closed carriage waited outside, Thomas on the box, Billy by the steps ready to hand Allegra in.

It was after 7.30; she was tardy. Allegra ran down the staircase, so busy watching her feet she forgot to pause and make the grand entrance she had planned.

Tremayne's eyes darkened and he had difficulty swallowing. 'My darling, you look *ravissante* tonight.' She held out her hands and he carried them to his lips, placing a kiss on each finger before releasing them.

'I am so glad you like this ensemble. This is its first airing. I have been saving it for an important occasion.'

'And a supper and card party count as such? It should have been kept for a ball.'

'No, Silas, my love, it is not the event but the venue. Tonight I am taking you to meet the Dowager Duchess of Avondale. If you can charm her, then all doors will open like magic to you. You will be received everywhere.'

Abbot arranged the cloak across Allegra's shoulders and they were ready to depart. Once they were settled he continued the conversation. 'I shall do my best tonight, Allegra, but I cannot promise it will be enough. I am not good at being a sycophant; breeding counts for nothing in my business world. I'm only impressed by achievements, not pedigrees.'

'I know you are. But the *haut ton* are not. I thought it was your goal to be part of society?'

He grinned, a flash of white in the gloom. 'I thought it was too, my love, but now I find that I don't give a damn . . . ' He sensed the maid's shocked recoil. 'I shall rephrase that. I do not care overmuch for society's opinion. If I have your approval, then that is more than enough for me.'

'In which case, my love, we can both relax and enjoy ourselves. I have never cared a fig for their opinion. My only concern is for you.'

The carriage finally halted outside the flambeaux-lit portico of their destination.

Two footmen attended their descent and two more ushered them upstairs.

'We would have been quicker to walk here; it has taken over thirty minutes to travel around the square,' Tremayne commented.

'Shall we walk back? When Thomas returns with the carriage he can arrange for an escort to be waiting outside when we leave.'

'I think in the present circumstances it would be better not.'

Allegra shivered at the unpleasant reminder that the mastermind behind the ambush was still at large.

*   *   *

The evening, an intimate gathering of twenty couples, sped by. Her friends owned themselves to be delighted to see her again and to meet her charming fiancé. Allegra shone with a radiance that illuminated the room. It was so long since she had had the opportunity to converse with like-minded people, to hear the latest *on-dits*, discuss the progress of the war, and bemoan the high price of corn.

At such an event there was not the vapid conversation of simpering debutantes. Discussions between both ladies and gentlemen were robust and stimulating. Tremayne's opinion on matters financial was sought and his views respected. In all they both declared themselves well satisfied with the evening.

'Almost dawn, Silas. It hardly seems worth the trouble of going to bed.'

He briefly squeezed her hands. 'You have more stamina than I, my sweet, I'm exhausted. Go in now; I shall call round in the afternoon. I have business to attend to this morning. Goodnight, my darling.'

★　★　★

He waited till Allegra and her maid had vanished inside before striding off to his own house, five minutes' walk away. High society was less objectionable than he had anticipated — in fact he rather thought he might come to enjoy their company. However, his first priority must be to discover why they had been attacked. He hoped that the men he had employed would return with sufficient information this morning to start piecing the puzzle together. So far the only suspect was his ex-mistress, Camille Oliver. But he knew her to be a pragmatist. She never did anything unless it would be of direct benefit to her in some way.

The death of either Demelza or Allegra could not come into that category, unless . . . ? He needed to think this through, analyse the situation. If Allegra was dead would he ever consider going back to his mistress? If he was honest he knew that he probably would, eventually. He had physical needs and Camille certainly knew how to satisfy those.

He rubbed his eyes; fatigue was making him over fanciful. Of course she was not behind the attacks, she was a woman, for God's sake! How could she possibly be involved with such a heinous crime? He needed his bed. He was not thinking clearly.

A drowsy footman answered his knock and bowed deeply, and barely concealing his yawn, delivered the message he had been given earlier. 'Good evening, sir. I have to tell you that Lord Witherton and a guest arrived just after you left this evening. They have been accommodated in the green suite.'

Tremayne nodded. He was glad Richard was here; perhaps together they could make sense of the situation. It seemed that the guest was Pledger; he was not so sure about his arrival.

★　★　★

'Is Lady Allegra awake yet, Miss Murrell? I am eager to hear what happened last night. I shall get up, I think, and go and see for myself.'

'Miss Demelza, Lady Allegra did not retire until the small hours so we should not expect to see her before noon. Also, Dr Canning gave instructions that you were to rest for another day.'

'I'm going mad with boredom cooped up in here. I shall get dressed and go for walk around the house. I promise I shall walk slowly.'

Her companion accepted defeat. 'I shall accompany you, my dear. This is a vast establishment. And an unwary guest could easily get themselves lost without directions.'

Demelza was admiring the spacious entrance hall, its walls lined with gloomy portraits of illustrious Witherton ancestors, when there was a sharp knock on the front door. It would not do for a visitor to see them lurking in the hall so Miss Murrell took Demelza's arm and began to bustle her towards a small ante-room to the right of the door. They were too late. The visitors were being ushered inside.

'Richard! You have come.' Demelza snatched her arm away and ran towards him and fell into his embrace. They kissed, to Miss Murrell's horror and Captain Pledger's amusement.

Demelza raised her head to gaze at Richard. 'Your poor face; does it hurt very much, my love?' Her fingers traced the lines of red that led up to the rakish black patch that covered his mangled eye.

'Hardly at all, my darling. And your shoulder, how is that?'

'A little sore, but it is healing well. We are both scarred now. I said right from the outset we would be a perfect match.'

'Demelza, I must introduce you to a good friend of mine. He rode through the night to fetch me to your side.' His arm still about her waist he swung around. 'This is Captain Gideon Pledger — Gideon, this is Miss Demelza Tremayne.'

She curtsied, he bowed, and all three retired to the main salon, on the first floor, to continue their conversation. Miss Murrell followed; engaged or not, Lord Witherton and Demelza should not be left unchaperoned.

★   ★   ★

Allegra, on hearing that her brother had arrived, flew through her *toilette* and hastened to the salon to greet him. As she walked in she realized Richard and Demelza were joyfully reunited, their mutual fears unfounded. 'Richard, I am so glad to see you here, and both of you so happy.'

Brother and sister embraced. 'I was worried unnecessarily; we both were. As soon as she is fully restored I wish to escort her to a party or two; there are still some left to attend, I hope, Allegra?'

'There are, Richard, my dear. We shall go together. Silas and I went to meet the Dowager Duchess of Avondale last evening and he has her stamp of approval. I am certain Demelza will be equally well received.'

★ ★ ★

It was here that Tremayne found them, Allegra laughing and happy in the company of the man she professed to dislike, her reservations quite obviously evaporated. His face was grim as he watched her rise and come towards him.

'Welcome, Silas. I do not believe you have been introduced to Richard's friend, Captain Pledger?'

He continued to stare, his eyes granite hard, his enmity plain, but did not answer or acknowledge the captain's bow. Finally the captain got the message and, half-bowing nervously to Allegra, mumbled an unintelligible farewell and disappeared through the door.

'I wish to speak to you in private, Allegra.'

She was startled by his tone and she stepped away. 'Of course. Shall we go to the small sitting room?'

Once inside Tremayne closed the door and stood with his back to it. Allegra felt the first stirring of unease. What was wrong? Why was Silas glaring at her?

'What is it, Silas? What have I done to offend you?'

'Perhaps you should tell me, Lady Allegra? What is that man to you? I believe there is a history between you, that you have not dared share with me.'

Allegra began to understand the direction of his questions. 'We have no history. He is a friend of Richard's. He was never a friend of mine, I can assure you of that.'

Tremayne stepped away from the door, his expression deadly. 'It's all over town. That he was your lover whilst he lived in your house. Is everything you have told me a lie? Are you not the innocent you purport to be? Why else would you be closeted alone with him at the White Hart the other night?'

Allegra did not dignify his accusation with an answer. Instead she calmly looked around for something to throw. Her fingers curled around a bronze statue and her arm went back, and she flung it across the room. Her aim was as accurate as it had been two days before.

Tremayne receiving the object full in the

chest reeled back, the breath squeezed from his lungs, and, gasping like a landed fish, crashed to the floor. Allegra stepped over him as if he wasn't there, and vanished, apparently unmoved, from the room.

17

'Abbott, where are you? I am going out. I need your assistance immediately,' Allegra called, as she ran into her bedroom. Strangely, her fury at Silas's unjust accusation was no longer uppermost in her mind. She wanted to know who had started these vicious rumours and the person who could tell her was Captain Pledger himself.

Five minutes after arriving in her chamber she left, by the backstairs, her maid close behind. Allegra had explained to Abbott what had happened and why they were going out as they descended the narrow, uncarpeted stairs.

The servants' exit at the rear of the house was deserted and they were able to slip out unobserved. 'Mr Tremayne's house is but a few minutes' walk. We do not need to attract attention to ourselves by haste. We will not be pursued, at least not yet.'

Her mouth curved as she recalled the look of stupefaction on the face of her beloved as he clutched his chest and toppled to the floor. It served him right. He deserved to suffer for allowing his jealousy to overcome his innate common sense. She intended to forgive him, eventually, but he would have to do a vast amount of grovelling before that time came.

'It is the next house, the one with a double front, and the navy painted door,' she told her abigail. At the bottom of the steps she paused, not sure how to proceed. She had never been in quite this situation before. Whenever she went visiting a footman accompanied her and was there to demand entry on her behalf.

'I think you had better go up, Abbott. I shall wait here.'

Her maid marched up the stone flight and banged the brass knocker loudly. The door swung open instantly. 'Lady Allegra Humphry wishes to speak to Captain Pledger who is residing here as a guest.'

The footman covered his surprise at such odd goings-on and bowed. 'Please come in, your ladyship. I shall send for the house-keeper to attend you immediately.'

Allegra looked around with interest — after all this would soon be her house as well. It was the same age and style as Witherton House but there the similarities ended for this abode was immaculate, having the most expensive and luxurious appointments she had ever seen. She rather thought the livery of the footman could have cost more than her own gown.

'If you would care to wait in the morning-room, my lady?' The footman ushered her into a nearby chamber. This was furnished in the latest fashion. The elegant furniture, some in satinwood, other items of mahogany, would have been made especially for the house by someone as prestigious as Thomas Chippendale or Hope if she was not mistaken. She much admired the rattan chair seats and their lacquer decorations.

She had not imagined Silas to be a man much influenced by fashion, but if this house was anything to go by he certainly liked to be up-to-date. Allegra wandered across the expanse of carpet feeling her boots sink pleasantly into the deep pile. The pale green-striped damask wall covering was repeated in the heavy curtains and swags at the windows, but she did not notice that. She was staring out of the window, watching the pedestrians, hoping she would have time enough to complete her mission before either Silas or Richard appeared to interfere.

She patted her reticule, her fingers pressing the hard shape of her pistol. It was always as well to come prepared. 'Abbott, could you go and see what is keeping Captain Pledger; if he does not come down then I shall go in search of him.'

'You must not, my lady. I shall go, if you wait here; I shall be but a moment.' Her maid hurried out to pass on the urgent message.

Allegra followed her to the open door and spotted her quarry coming downstairs his carpetbag in his hand. He was leaving. She would not allow that to happen. Without thought to the consequences she rushed out, blocking his exit.

'Captain Pledger, I wish to speak with you.'

He tried to step around her but she moved too fast.

'I am pressed for time, Lady Allegra. I beg your pardon, but I have urgent business elsewhere.'

'You are going nowhere until you have answered my questions, sir.'

Believing she would not dare to speak of anything contentious he half bowed, a sneer curling his lips. 'Then I am your servant, my lady. Please ask what you will.'

She pulled herself up to her full height, not much shorter than his, and narrow-eyed, raked him from head to toe. He flushed under her bitter scrutiny. 'Are you the fabricator of the malicious gossip that is racing around town?'

'What gossip would that be?'

'That you and I were lovers, sir. That is the gossip I refer to.'

He recoiled slightly at her tone. 'Now why should I wish to spread such tales? I have nothing to gain from it; my reputation is as besmirched as yours.'

That had a certain logic. Was she, like Silas, being too quick to judge? 'Then who, Captain Pledger, if it was not you?'

He bared his teeth in a false smile. 'Lady Oliver, your betrothed's mistress. It is she who will gain if Tremayne leaves you. He will return to her and she wants him back at any price.' He leaned closer and lowered his voice. 'She is a woman who knows how to please a man. She is not a cold bitch like you. Tremayne will return to her warm bed, never doubt it, my lady. Camille Oliver can give him something you are not capable of.'

Allegra, during this shocking speech, had covertly slipped her hand into her reticule and gripped the butt of her pistol. Slowly, not wishing to alarm him, she withdrew her gun and with it concealed behind her back, she took two steps back. With calm deliberation she raised it and watched his expression change from triumph to abject fear. 'You are a hair's breadth from eternity, sir. I suggest you leave this house and this vicinity before I change my mind and pull the trigger.'

They were both unaware that this scenario

was being watched by the housekeeper, Adamson the butler, two footmen and a parlour-maid.

He did not have to be told twice, but turned and fled across the marble floor, his portmanteau swinging wildly in his hand. A footman reacted swiftly and politely bowed him out but, in his astonishment, neglected to close the door.

Allegra replaced the unloaded gun in her bag, well satisfied with the outcome of her encounter. She had the information she required; she knew who had been behind the attempted assassination. She could not wait to see the expression on the face of her fiance when she mentioned the name of his mistress, Lady Oliver, to him.

She smiled sunnily at the housekeeper. 'Is there a garden room in which I can wait?'

'Yes, my lady. I shall conduct you there.'

Allegra turned to Adamson. 'I am expecting Mr Tremayne and Lord Witherton to arrive at any moment. Please inform them of my whereabouts.'

'Would you like some refreshments sent in, my lady?' The housekeeper's voice was a trifle unsteady.

'No, thank you, not now. But please send in the brandy decanter and glasses when the gentlemen arrive.'

Allegra found herself a comfortable chair close to the French doors and sat down. 'Abbott, I have an errand for you. I shall be quite safe sitting here so you need not look so disapproving.'

★ ★ ★

The sound of Tremayne's fall had been clearly audible throughout the adjacent rooms as he took a side table and its ornaments down with him. Richard was the first to arrive, but found himself unable to slide through the small gap from which Allegra had exited. The door wouldn't budge. He put his shoulder to it and pushed.

'What is that strange gurgling noise, Richard, and why can't you open the door?'

'I have no idea, Demelza. Are you able to slide through that gap, do you think, without further damaging your shoulder?'

She eyed it dubiously. 'I shall try. But you must push hard as I do so.'

Richard gripped the door edge and threw his weight forward; the door moved a fraction, giving sufficient space for her to slip into the room. She stared in dismay at her father, sprawled on the floor, clutching his chest.

'Papa, whatever is wrong? Are you unwell?'

Her immediate consideration was that he was suffering from apoplexy. 'Richard, my father is taken very ill; he is behind the door, blocking your entrance.'

Richard renewed his efforts but the door wouldn't shift. He needed more weight. 'You two, get over here and assist me,' he shouted at the watching footmen. Willingly the young men added their bulk and slowly the door began to move. 'Stop, that is enough.' Richard squeezed through the gap and dropped to his knees beside Demelza, who was holding Tremayne's hand, not sure what to do for the best.

Richard feared the worst. It was tragic to see a man in his prime struck down in this way. He took the other hand. He realized there was little even a physician could do to help Tremayne. They must offer what comfort they could in his final minutes.

'My darling, you must be brave, I believe he has not long to live.'

She nodded, her tears dripping unheeded on to her father's crisp white neck-cloth. 'Papa, can you speak to me? Is there anything you want to say?'

Tremayne finally recovered his voice and the ability to move. He snatched his hands away and pushed himself up to seated position. 'For God's sake, I'm not about to turn up my toes. I was temporarily winded, not dying.'

'You were not having an apoplexy?' She sounded almost disappointed. 'Then why were you gobbling like a turkey and unable to move?'

'Allegra threw a bronze figure at me and it caught me full in the chest. Here, lad, give me your arm, I don't wish to languish on the floor a moment longer.'

Richard heaved and Tremayne, his back against the door, slowly shuffled his feet until he was upright. Demelza, dry-eyed, faced him.

'Exactly what did you say to Allegra, Papa?'

Tremayne flushed and couldn't meet her gaze. 'I asked her if Pledger had been her lover.' A shocked silence greeted this statement.

'How could you say such a dreadful thing? It is no wonder Allegra threw something at you. You're a disgrace. I am ashamed to call you my father.' With those damning words she rushed from the room determined to find, and comfort, her dear friend.

Richard glared at his future father-in-law and his fists bunched. 'Sir, if Allegra had not already felled you, then I would do so myself.'

Tremayne raised his hands, palms upward. 'Please do so, if it will make you feel any better. I deserve to be horse-whipped for saying such a thing.'

Richard lowered his fists. 'Then why did you say it? What prompted you to accuse her of such base behaviour?'

'I need to sit down, lad. I still feel a little shaky.' He raised a warning hand. 'No, I can manage.' Once seated he dropped his head into his hands with a groan of despair. 'I am famous for my clear thinking; indeed I have built my business around my ability to recognize false dealings, not to be taken in by a dissembler. I cannot imagine what maggot got into my brain today.' He was silent, his ragged breathing the only sound in the room. 'I have no excuse — none at all. If I have lost Allegra's love, then I have only myself to blame.'

'Tell me, why did you do it? If you can explain your motives satisfactorily to me, then it is possible that Allegra will understand also.'

Tremayne sat up. 'I went to White's and found myself greeted by strange looks and sympathetic pats on the back. Eventually I persuaded someone to explain.'

'Go on, sir.'

'It's all over town; everyone is talking about the fact that Allegra and Pledger were lovers whilst he lived at the Priory. That he was so overcome by grief when she dismissed him that he departed leaving half his belongings behind. That she met with him alone in her parlour at the White Hart to make arrangements to renew the relationship after our marriage.' He stopped to gauge his listener's reaction. 'There is some truth in this, is there not?'

Richard nodded, his expression grave. 'Enough to give the story credence. I must hear the rest, pray continue, sir.'

'The gossip has it that she decided she would set her cap at me, having sent Pledger packing before I arrived. It seemed to fit so well. I came round here, not to accuse her, you understand, but to sift the truth from the lies. When I walked in to find Allegra cosying up to the man she had told me she disliked above all others I was insane with jealousy.'

Richard could see why Tremayne might have reacted as he did. It was possible he would have done so himself in similar circumstances. 'You were blinded by your suspicion and spoke without thought.'

'I did. I knew I was making a catastrophic error even as the words were passing my lips. Allegra's face told me all I needed to know.' He grinned, his expression rueful. 'She was not upset, not the slightest bit embarrassed, but angry. I consider myself lucky she did not have a pistol to hand, or my injuries could have proved fatal.'

'Poor Allegra. She is of unassailable purity; she has never flirted, never so much as held the hand of a gentleman, apart from myself and our father. To accuse her of something so base was mistaking her character in such a way that it is hardly surprising she reacted with violence.' Richard chuckled. 'It is extraordinary — my sister has always been the calm, sensible twin. I cannot imagine what has caused her to change so radically.'

'Love can do strange things to a person unused to the emotion. Good God! Look at me — I have become as irrational and muddleheaded as she is.' He winced when he laughed. 'I think I might have broken a rib. But I shall not complain. It is my just desserts. How long you think it will take for her to forgive me?'

Before Richard could answer they heard Demelza returning. 'Allegra is not in her rooms. Jenny says she ran in and stayed only long enough to put on her spencer, bonnet and gloves, then rushed off again.'

Tremayne pushed himself upright using the arms of the chair as levers. 'Where will she have gone, Witherton?'

Richard frowned, then his face cleared. 'To your house, to find Captain Pledger. This gossip had to emanate from him; no one else could possibly have such precise information. But why he should wish to ruin Allegra's reputation in this way I have no idea.'

Demelza knew, or she thought she did. 'You told me that he offered for her and she turned him down. I imagine, for some gentlemen, being rejected would be an unacceptable dent to their pride.'

'God in his heaven! Are you saying she's going to accuse him of ruining her, Witherton?'

'I am. It is her way; it always has been. She takes things head on, no prevaricating.'

Tremayne moved with a speed that belied his injury. 'Come with me, we must find her. If Pledger holds the kind of grudge that Demelza is suggesting, she could find herself in serious difficulties.'

With Richard in close pursuit, he took the stairs two at a time. The footman, on guard at the front door, barely had time to throw it open. As they pounded down the pavement, shoulder to shoulder, dodging the pedestrians, and occasioning not a few raised eyebrows, Richard said what they were both thinking.

'If Allegra has taken a pistol, I do not think much of Pledger's chances. Anything could happen.'

Tremayne was having difficulty breathing, his chest felt as if a red-hot poker was being forced in to it. He shook his head, his breath whistling strangely in his throat, unable to respond in any other way. When he saw his front door stood open he feared the worst. He staggered up the steps and burst into the hall. His butler, Adamson, received his second shock of the morning.

The man appeared to be waiting for them, a slightly bemused expression on his normally impassive face. 'Mr Tremayne, your lordship, Lady Allegra is in the garden-room.'

'And Pledger, where is he?' Tremayne managed to gasp.

'He has departed, sir, a few minutes ago.'

Richard, realizing Tremayne's difficulty, stepped in. 'What has taken place here? Tell us quickly.'

'Lady Allegra and Captain Pledger had words, sir. Lady Allegra threatened to shoot Captain Pledger and he ran away.' The speech was delivered with a degree of satisfaction.

Tremayne grabbed Richard's arm for support, his tortured breathing subsiding, finally allowing him to speak. 'I told you, lad; that sister of yours is fearsome. The sooner I get her back to Essex and safely married the happier I shall be.'

At the rear of the house he found his

beloved calmly watching the antics of a pair of squirrels on the lawn. In the excitement, and relief, he had temporarily forgotten he was in disgrace. She had not.

The look she gave him would have curdled milk. 'Mr Tremayne, how good to see you. And Richard; is Demelza to arrive at any moment also?'

Tremayne cleared his throat, his glance not quite meeting hers. 'I owe you an apology. Are you prepared to accept it?'

Richard seeing the twinkle in his sister's eyes smiled and left the room, quietly closing the door behind him.

'Please feel free to be seated, sir. Have you nothing else to add?' He looked warily around the room and she understood his concern. 'My pistol is not loaded, sir, you are quite safe from harm.'

He snatched a spindle-legged, cane-seated chair and straddled it. 'I am sincerely relieved to hear that, my dear. I do not wish to add a bullet hole to my broken ribs.'

She snorted inelegantly. 'It serves you right, Silas. How could you have thought, for a second, that I had shared my bed with that . . . with that obnoxious coxcomb?'

'My brain was addled by jealousy. That is no excuse, I know. I shall sit here and give you my full permission to throw whatever missiles come to hand, I know I deserve it.'

'Silas, you are impossible! I have no intention of throwing anything at you ever again. But you must promise never to accuse me of such a terrible thing.'

'Of course I promise. But I am becoming concerned that you appear to have suddenly developed a penchant for violence, my love. When I proposed to you I believed you to be calm and dignified, a woman to be admired not feared. Shall I be safe in your hands, or live in daily fear of execution?'

She laughed out loud at his performance. 'I can promise you, Silas, that if no one else tries to shoot a close member of my family, or accuse me of being impure, then I shall not be tempted to resort to violence.' Her smile faded and she paled. 'I did not mean to kill that man. It was an instinctive reaction because he had hurt my darling Demelza. I wished merely to retaliate.'

He surged to his feet, his chair falling to the floor, and dropped to his knees beside her. 'Sweetheart, if you had not killed him, and I would have done so. It was well done, for I hate a shoddy job. And remember, if he had survived he would have ended his miserable life dangling on the end of a rope. Surely it is better for his parents to believe him murdered by footpads than to watch him die on the gallows?'

'But that does not change the fact that I am a murderer. I have blood on my hands. How can you bear to touch me after what I have done?'

In answer he drew her down beside him and slid his arms around her. 'I love you, Allegra. There is nothing you have done or could ever do that could change that.'

She put one hand around his neck and lifted up her face to receive his kiss. As the blood roared in her ears, her doubts vanished to be replaced by sensations of a different, and delightful, kind.

It was Tremayne who pulled back before it was too late. Gently he removed her hands from his neck and lifted her back to her seat. Her mouth was swollen from his kisses, her normally pale cheeks hectic with colour. It was only then he noticed the absence of her maid.

'Allegra, don't tell me you came here unaccompanied? Where is your abigail?'

'I have sent her out on an errand, Silas.' She giggled. 'I rather think, in the circumstances, it is a good thing she was not in here.'

Awkwardly, he regained his feet, his right hand held to his sternum. Instantly her amusement changed to anxiety. 'Silas, are you in pain? I am so sorry. I did not realize I had thrown that statue with such force. It must be because I have played cricket since I was a girl. My father taught me to throw fast and with accuracy.'

'This is nothing, forget it, my dear. Now we tell me, where is Abbott?'

'I sent her to visit a cousin of hers, who is cook at Lady Marshall's establishment on the other side of the square. I wish to know how far the gossip has spread. If it is already kitchen talk it is too late to put things right. We are both ruined. For myself, I do not care over much; it is you I am concerned for.'

'I told you yesterday that if I have your approval I care naught for anyone else. And I rather think both Witherton and Demelza will feel the same.'

'I hope so. But I forgot, in the excitement, to tell you what I discovered.' She stared straight at him as she spoke. 'I believe it is an old friend of yours, one Lady Oliver, who is behind all this. It would seem that she wants you back and is prepared to go to any lengths to achieve her objective.'

Quite unabashed, he nodded. 'Your information dovetails with mine. My informants told me she had recently sold an expensive piece of jewellery for cash. That money could have been used to pay the men who tried to kill you.'

Allegra was still perplexed. Something was not quite right with this story. 'But how could she have known the lieutenant that I shot? Where could she have made this contact?'

Tremayne, already on his feet, paced the floor, thinking hard before he answered. 'God's teeth! We have missed the obvious.'

'What, Silas? What have we missed?'

'How did Pledger know Lady Oliver was the gossipmonger? How could she have had all the details, unless he had given them to her?'

She understood his direction and her eyes rounded with horror. 'Who better to find soldiers to do his dirty work than another soldier?'

'Exactly. You were right to suspect him all along. It is Captain Pledger that we seek. It has to have been a joint effort. Lady Oliver supplied the funds and he organized the attempt.'

He walked to the door and, opening it, shouted down the corridor, further startling the ever-attentive footman waiting outside. 'Richard, where are you, man? We have plans to make.'

18

The butler appeared, his brow creased. 'I'm afraid that Lord Witherton is not here, sir. He left a moment ago.'

Tremayne swore under his breath. 'Did he say where he was going, Adamson?'

'I believe he went to fetch Miss Tremayne, sir.'

'Very well. Have them join us in the garden-room when they arrive.'

Allegra met him at the door. 'Where is Richard?'

'Gone to fetch Demelza, but God knows what for.'

She slipped her arm through his. 'Come in and sit down, Silas. We have things to talk about and might not get another opportunity.' She tugged, insisting he followed her. 'Scowling down the corridor will not produce them — it will just give you a headache, my dear.'

The green warmth of the garden beckoned and they decided it would be pleasurable to stroll whilst they conversed.

'There is one thing about all this I do not understand,' Allegra said. 'Why should

Pledger wish to kill me? I did no more than refuse his offer, hardly enough to warrant assassination.'

'It is something I have also considered.'

'And?' Allegra prompted impatiently.

'I have only one explanation. The man must be deranged.' At first she thought he was funning and she smiled, then she saw his face. 'The actions of a sane man can be predicted, anticipated, but a madman, by his very nature, will behave irrationally.'

'I understand. If he was, well, normally motivated, what would you expect him to do next?'

'If it was me, I would report to Horse Guards and ask to be posted to the Americas. He must realize he has been discovered, that his days of freedom are rapidly diminishing.'

Allegra walked over to smell the pungent honeysuckle and his eyes followed her. She glanced up, her lips curving in a smile. 'Do not look so fierce, my love; whatever he does I am certain you and Richard will find him before he can do any more harm.'

He closed the space between them in one stride. 'Allegra, I love you. I do not know why you return my regard, but I thank God that you do.'

'Do you not? Could it be the fact that you are not only one of the warmest men in

England but also the most attractive?'

Her gurgle of amusement was swallowed by his fierce kiss. Several intoxicating minutes later she emerged, breathless, and more than a little dishevelled. 'My bonnet ribbons are strangling me, Silas. Could you release them for me?'

With expert fingers he undid the knotted ribbon and tossed the hat aside. It landed neatly on the head of a Greek cherub standing in a nearby arbour. Allegra clapped her hands.

'Bravo! That was an excellent shot — I could not have done better myself.'

Chuckling he took her hand and kissed it. 'Shall we sit over there, on the bench, where it's shaded?'

'And you shall restore my bonnet to me, Silas. Abbott will be extremely disapproving if she returns to find me so undressed.' She quickly placed a warning finger on his lips. 'No, my dear, you must not use a profanity. I asked you to mend your language and you promised me you would do so.'

Restoring the bonnet was a pleasurable experience for both and it was there that Richard and Demelza found them later.

'Oh, Papa, Allegra has forgiven you already. I would not have done so, I can assure you, for another day at least.'

Tremayne embraced his daughter and grinned sheepishly at Richard. 'I am glad you're back; we have important matters to discuss.'

'I thought Demelza would be beside herself with anxiety, so brought her here to see that all is well.'

'We are both well and our differences forgotten. Now, Witherton and I have plans to make; Demelza, you stay and keep Allegra company.' He turned and, with his hand on Richard's shoulder, guided him back inside the house.

'What are they going to do, Allegra? Did my father tell you?'

Allegra realized that he had not, in fact, done so. 'I think he intends to find Captain Pledger and Lady Oliver and have them apprehended. But how, or where, I have no idea.'

To her astonishment Demelza headed for the French doors, her face determined. 'Richard is not leaving without telling me where he is going. And neither is Papa.'

When, a few moments later, Allegra decided to follow, not quite sure how their unlooked for appearance would be viewed by either Silas or Richard, she discovered that the garden-room was empty. Where had they all gone? She could hear raised voices somewhere in the house and hurried in that direction.

In the spacious hall Demelza was hanging on to Richard's arm, berating him loudly. Of Silas there was no sign. Conscious that the staff were being given more excitement in one afternoon than they normally had in a year, she hurried over to intervene.

'Enough of this. Demelza, be silent at once.' Her voice was quiet but firm. 'Richard what is all this fuss about? Are you both aware that you are making a spectacle of yourselves?'

Demelza dropped her hand and her shoulders drooped in defeat. Without another word she turned and fled up the stairs to seek sanctuary in the rooms she had previously occupied on her visits to the capital.

Richard groaned. 'She does not think I am well enough to accompany Tremayne. But I have no choice, Sis, I am honour bound to go. For the man's bullet was meant for you and it hit my fiancée.'

'I understand, and when I have spoken to her, I am certain that Demelza will also. Where is Silas?'

'Two men have recently arrived with news. He has gone to speak with them.'

'Shall we go back into the garden-room? You can tell me what is to happen.'

Once they were comfortably settled Allegra looked expectantly at her brother. 'Well, Richard? What is Silas planning to do? Did he tell you he thinks that Captain Pledger is insane?'

'He did and I am afraid I have to agree. There can be no other explanation. He is like a thwarted child wishing to destroy what he cannot have for himself.' His mouth turned down and his expression was sombre. 'I have known Gideon since we were at school and never suspected he was unstable. I cannot imagine what has turned his mind in this way.'

'I think I can. I believe that he has harboured an obsession for me all these years and when I rejected him so brutally, the coin spun and love became hate. I never liked him, as you are aware, but I am saddened by the thought that one of England's heroes has come to this because of me.' She stopped, lost in thought. 'Will he go to the gallows when he is caught?'

Richard shook his head. 'Not if I can help it. A quick end — it is the least I can do for an old friend.'

She shuddered. 'Perhaps he will take the honourable way out, or make his escape to France?' Despite her disquiet she half smiled. 'Do you know, Richard, that I asked Fred to arrange for me to meet with a free-trader? I wanted Silas to be abducted, taken to France, so that he would miss the day of our wedding and release both of us from those contracts.'

'Good God! It is not only Pledger who has run mad! What did Fred say?'

'He assumed that I wanted to arrange for a delivery of cognac and tea and insisted that it would be unnecessary for me to speak directly to the smugglers. I could hardly tell him otherwise, now could I?' She smiled at Richard. 'I promise I would not have gone through with it. I was angry that day, but by the following morning I was greatly relieved I had not been able to arrange anything of the sort.'

'Did we get the brandy and tea?'

'I have no idea. I had forgotten all about it until you mentioned France.'

Richard tried to appear disapproving. 'I am supposed to be setting a good example in the community not fraternizing with free-traders and receiving contraband.'

Tremayne came in to join them. 'Good, I'm glad you are both here. I have heard from Forsythe; you remember, Allegra, the gentleman who assisted us at the White Hart the other night?' Allegra's smile slipped she recalled why the gentleman had been obliged to help.

He continued, 'It appears that there are three men absent without leave from Colchester barracks. The lieutenant we know about, but also a sergeant and an enlisted man. I have the names and descriptions of both.'

Richard interrupted. 'There were two men with information, were they both from Forsythe?'

'No, the second was a Bow Street runner in my employment. He has discovered that Lady Oliver owns a small estate, inherited from a maternal relation of her late husband. It is in a small village not far from Ipswich. It is my guess they are all holed up there.'

'In that case we can travel back together, Silas. I wish to return to the Priory. I have no intention of attending any further society events until the gossip has died down and the truth is known.'

'I was going to suggest exactly that, my love. I should be happier escorting you and Demelza myself.' He glanced at Richard. 'We are to meet up with an escort from the barracks when we get to Colchester. They want those men back; they don't take kindly to deserters.'

Allegra got to her feet. 'I was about to remove my bonnet, yet again,' she said, blushing rosily at Tremayne's grin, 'but I rather think I had better collect Demelza. If we are intending to leave at first light tomorrow, there is a deal of packing for us to organize. I can explain to her what is happening at the same time.'

'We shall take the journey back gently; there is no urgency. My men are watching Grafton Manor, Lady Oliver's house, no one will be allowed to leave before we arrive.'

'It is scarcely two hours' ride to Grafton from Colchester. We can be there and back in the day,' Richard added.

Allegra moved to the door. 'Are we to break our journey at the Saracen's Head, in Chelmsford, Silas, where we stayed on the way up?'

'Yes. I shall send someone ahead to reserve our accommodation. We must leave at the crack of dawn. We can break our fast at the White Hart in Romford. I'm sure Mrs Foster will be pleased to see that Demelza is fully recovered.'

★ ★ ★

At six o'clock the following morning a small cavalcade left Witherton House. Tremayne had decided that the diligence, containing luggage, should travel with their carriage, and two extra grooms were to follow as outriders.

The interior of the carriage, with two large gentleman and three ladies inside, was a shade overcrowded, but neither Allegra nor Demelza objected to being obliged to sit thigh to thigh with their betrotheds. Miss Murrell was forced to be an unwilling observer and official chaperon and felt decidedly *de trop*.

Tremayne and Richard accompanied the ladies all the way to the Priory in order to collect their own mounts from the stables.

'Take care, Silas, my love. I know there will be a troop of soldiers with you, and there are only three of them, but if they are aware that their capture is imminent, they could fight to the death. They have nothing to lose after all.' She shivered as she remembered Richard's promise, that he would not allow his erstwhile friend to suffer the indignity of the rope.

Silas smoothed an errant strand of pale-gold hair from her face with tender fingers. 'I am not foolhardy, my darling. I have too much to live for to risk my life unnecessarily. But until these men, and Lady Oliver, are apprehended I cannot rest easy.'

She stretched up and touched his mouth with hers, her eyes soft with love. 'Look after Richard, remember his vision is impaired.'

'I will; I shall remain at his right shoulder throughout.'

The two men were to rendezvous with the military party at Ardleigh, a ride of only a few miles. She watched them canter, side by side, down the drive and across the park until they were lost from view.

'Come along, Demelza, let us go inside. I am sure that they will come to no harm. They could even be back before supper, I am certain of it.'

★ ★ ★

Tremayne and his escort had travelled scarcely five miles when they spotted two horsemen galloping towards them. The lead rider wrenched his mount to a halt.

'Thank God we have caught you, Mr Tremayne. The bastards have slipped through the net. They were there earlier; we saw them through the spyglass in the stable yard, but when we checked later their mounts had gone.'

Tremayne's brow creased. 'Did Captain Pledger arrive there last night?'

'No, sir, nobody came. Lady Oliver did receive a message, but she did not go out. She is still in residence.'

He swore. 'God damn it to hell! They are meeting him somewhere. But where?'

'The coast?' Richard suggested. 'It is a high

tide tonight and a smuggler's moon. The ideal time to slip aboard a ship and sail to freedom.'

'You know the area, lad, which port will they head for?'

Richard did a rapid calculation. 'There is only one place where free-traders have never been caught — our own creek. There are legitimate wherries in and out as well as smugglers.'

Tremayne stood in his stirrups and shouted his command to the waiting troops. 'Lieutenant, the birds have flown. We believe they will head for the coast, try to catch a ship to France.' The troop, headed by Tremayne and Richard, and the two Bow Street runners close behind, swung round and galloped back the way they'd come.

★ ★ ★

It was almost dark and Allegra sat alone in the orangery, the glass doors open, enjoying the cool salty breeze that wafted from the creek. The birds were singing their final evening songs before settling down for the night. Demelza was safely in her room with Miss Murrell for company. All she had to do was wait. She had asked for a late supper to be served if Silas and Richard returned before ten o'clock. She would not hear them from where she was but a footman would run across to fetch her as soon as they arrived.

A slight noise outside in the garden startled her. Was there someone outside? Before she could raise the alarm a shadow slipped through the doors and her mouth was cruelly covered by an iron hand.

'One sound from you, my lady, and it will be your last.' Allegra swallowed convulsively, her teeth clenched shut, trying to push her head away from Captain Pledger's grip. She had no time to shout before a kerchief was tied tight around her mouth stifling any protests.

'Get up and do not struggle; I am quite prepared to break your arm. You are coming with me. I have arranged a cosy passage for us both in a Frenchie's boat. I hope you have no objection to life in France?' His laugh was manic causing the small hairs on the back of her neck to stiffen.

She tried to hang like a deadweight in his arms, but he twisted her wrist viciously up her back and she was forced to go with him. He half pushed, half dragged, her out into the night, towards the darkness of the trees that bordered the garden.

The dampness of the grass quickly soaked through her flimsy slippers and without the benefit of spencer or wrap she shivered in the cool night air. She saw a movement ahead, and two shadowy shapes detached themselves from the trees.

'I have her here. Bring the ropes, we must secure her. I do not trust her not to make a break for it.'

Allegra knew where she was being taken, towards the creek. It was high tide and it would be a simple matter to bring in a small rowing boat and transfer her to a larger vessel waiting in the deeper water. If no coastguard cutter was abroad to interfere they could slip anchor and sail away undetected. Silas! She would never see his dear face again. She was lost to him. He had ridden, unsuspecting, to Grafton leaving this monster to capture her. If she was to get free she had to do it herself: there was no one else to save her.

The cords that the two accomplices bound around her, bit into her bare arms and she knew it was useless to struggle. She would save her energy to make an escape attempt later. She let herself be dragged through the grounds to the greensward known as the Bury where the men had horses tethered under the huge tree. She was thrown, face down, across the pommel, and gagged as the sour stench of sweat filled her nostrils. She recognized the pungent odour: it meant that the horses were blown — they had been ridden to exhaustion.

If a rescue party did appear they could easily overtake her captors and secure her release. She prayed that someone would notice her absence, that a villager might glimpse her abduction. But she knew it was a false hope. It was a smuggler's moon, no villagers kept watch on a night like this. If an excise officer made enquiries about contraband they had no need to lie. They saw nothing pass their cottages; they never did, not when high tide and moonlight coincided.

She was grateful the ride was short, hanging head down made her feel decidedly sick.

'Is the boat there? Can you see it?' Pledger hissed, as he struggled to lift Allegra from across his saddle.

'It is, Captain, and I can see the Frenchie's vessel in the channel. They have the sails unfurled; we do not have long to get aboard.'

'Here, help me carry her ladyship. She is a deadweight; I believe she has swooned.'

Allegra forced her limbs to remain limp as the three men stumbled across the marshy grass to the water's edge their boots squelching loudly in the silence. She could smell the sea, hear the small waves slapping on the boat's sides. She didn't dare open her eyes to get a clearer look, they might, despite their hurry, realize she was faking her inertia.

Pledger swore under his breath as his boots filled with cold water. She shivered involuntarily as her skirts trailed in the sea and icy water travelled up the material to make it cling heavily to her legs. She opened her eyes. Was now the time to struggle, whilst they were attempting to put her into the rocking boat? She twisted violently, throwing the men off-balance, she felt herself dropping, then the sea engulfed her and her nose and mouth filled with salt water.

It was so cold. Numbingly cold. She was a good swimmer but with her arms bound she was unable to do more than attempt to place her feet on the slippery mud underfoot and try to stand up. She could hear the shouts and splashes of the men as they searched for her. She knew the water was less than hip deep, if she could stand up, maybe she could make good her escape in the darkness.

Then hands grabbed her and she was pulled sideways, away from the dinghy. Her lungs were bursting, and she could not hold her breath for much longer. A hand came round to uncover her mouth and her head broke the surface. She gulped in air whilst frantically trying to put down her feet. They didn't touch. She was out of her depth

— whoever had hold of her was towing her the wrong way, out to sea, not back to the safety of the shore.

She was freezing, the long skirts clinging to her legs making swimming impossible, but she could try. She would not give in without a fight.

'Keep still, darling, I have you safe.'

How could she not have known? Not recognized whose arms she was in? She relaxed instantly, too cold to answer, but Silas understood. He spoke directly into her ear, as he swam strongly, parallel to the shore. 'If we try and land too soon we will be seen. Richard's waiting further up.'

She was so cold; it was deadening her limbs, making it hard to think. She had to stay conscious, not allow Pledger to win, not now. Then she felt his feet touch the bottom and she was out of the water cradled in his arms. She thought she heard the rapid crack of gunfire, shouts and screams, but it was so hard to stay awake. She closed her eyes and let the darkness take her.

★ ★ ★

'Richard, I have her. She's unharmed, but half frozen.' He waited whilst Richard swung up into his saddle. 'Take care. Here, let me

318

wrap both our coats around her. I will be back as soon as this is over. Ride carefully, but as fast as you can. She needs to get warm. It is a matter of urgency.'

He didn't wait to see them go but dropped to the grass and forced his boots back on over his sodden stockings and breeches. He wanted to rejoin the small troop and discover if all the men were apprehended. He ran back along the shore towards the soldiers. The gunfire had ceased; he had not heard any return shots.

Movement in the channel attracted his attention, a vessel, sails up, was slinking out of the creek. God damnit! Were they too late? Had the men escaped them after all?

The lieutenant straightened as he heard his approach. 'We're all finished here, sir. No survivors. Two shot, one drowned.' His tone was even — it mattered little to him one way or the other.

Tremayne pushed his dripping hair from his eyes, his shirt sleeve a flash of white in the darkness. 'Excellent result, Lieutenant. Well done to you all. Lady Allegra's on her way back to the Priory. That is your half of the situation settled. The rest is up to me.'

He strode back to his horse, Apollo, patiently munching the scrubby grass that edged the creek, held by one of the Bow

Street runners. 'Wiggins, do you need my assistance to complete this night's work?'

'No, sir, we know what to do. We escort Lady Oliver to Harwich and put her on the first ship to have a free berth.'

'That's right. She can take any gold she has and her jewellery, and a maid, if one will agree to travel with her, but nothing else. Make sure she understands that if she sets foot in England again she will be arrested and hanged.'

'My pleasure, Mr Tremayne. It's not often that we get the chance to escort a flash mort like her. Beats murderers and thieves any day.'

'Good. Then be on your way, Wiggins. Report to me at the Priory when your task is completed successfully.'

Satisfied the matter was resolved, that his love was safe from further attack, he mounted and galloped the short distance back to the Priory. He had not liked the way Allegra's head had lolled against his shoulder or the icy chill of her limbs.

★ ★ ★

Allegra remained comatose throughout the desperate gallop back to the Priory, did not rouse even when stripped off by her maids and wrapped in warm red flannel. Her body's defences crumpled. The long immersion in the cold North Sea had been too much for her. She had nothing left to fight with. Her body temperature was so low that Dr Jones feared the worst.

'I'm sorry, my lord, there is nothing else we can do, apart from pray. If Lady Allegra's temperature does not start to rise soon then I fear she will die.'

Demelza's face contorted and Richard pulled her close. 'Allegra is strong, my love, she will pull through this. We must not give up hope yet.'

'I wish Papa was here. He would know what to do he always does.' Their heads turned as the sound of running feet approached Allegra's room. Silas rushed in, his hair wild, his clothes wet.

'How is she? Has she recovered consciousness?' He recoiled at the bleak faces. Doctor Jones? What was wrong?

'It is grave, sir. I fear her ladyship will not live to see the morning. Unless there is a miracle, I believe she will die.'

'Never! I shall not let that happen,' Tremayne snarled. 'Get out, all of you. I wish to be alone with her.'

Richard escorted the quietly crying Demelza from the bedchamber. Miss Murrell and the doctor followed. Tremayne turned angrily to Abbott and Jenny still hovering by the bedside.

'You, too, get out.'

They left, believing that there was no point in protecting Lady Allegra's reputation. As the door closed he began to strip off his soaking garments. His boots crashed to the floor, his shirt and breeches followed. Stark naked he gently unrolled the flannel that covered Allegra. His heart contracted when he felt her arms. Was he too late? He must not be. He could not let her die. Without her, his life would be over too.

He was hardly aware of her small breasts, her waist, or the way her hips flared out enticingly. He knew there was one chance to save her, one way he might get her warm. He climbed up on to the bed and, gathering her into his arms, rolled the red material back around them both, leaving one arm out to reach over and drag the winter comforter across.

He pulled her cold limp form hard against him, his legs curled round hers and his arms pressed her close; there was not an inch of her icy flesh that was not touching his naked warmth. He did not intend to sleep, but he had ridden hard, swum half a mile and exhaustion overtook him.

Soon the only sound in the bedchamber was that of his gentle breathing, hers was too shallow, too weak to be heard.

★　★　★

A delicious, unusual heat brought Allegra from her stupor; only half awake she revelled in the feeling. She had been so cold; she shivered as she recalled the icy drag of the sea on her clothes. Now she felt so safe, so contented, wrapped in the arms of the man she loved.

She stiffened. Surely not? She was imagining things — it was a lovely dream. Her eyes flickered open to meet his sleepy, navy-blue gaze.

'Good morning, my darling. You're looking much better today.'

'Silas! What are you doing in my bed?' It was then she realized neither of them were clothed. She felt heat suffuse her. 'You have no garments on.'

He smiled lazily. 'And neither do you, my love.' With slow deliberation he ran his hands up from the top of her legs to her shoulders. A quite different heat surged through her body.

'What are you doing? You must not.'

He nibbled her ear, sending shockwaves

through her. 'Why not, sweetheart? I have a special licence in my desk. We can be married this afternoon.'

She was finding it increasingly difficult to answer. 'But we are not married at this precise moment, are we?'

In answer to her question he dropped feather-light kisses along her jaw and then he claimed her mouth with his own. This time her lips parted allowing him unimpeded access to the inner moistness. When his hand slid round to cup her breast it swelled under his fingers. She guessed it was far too late to worry about proprieties.

He pulled away from her, his eyes questioning. 'Are you sure, my darling? If you want me to, I can wait.'

A sweet heaviness was holding her captive, making it difficult to open her eyes, to find the strength to answer. 'But I realize that I cannot. I want to be yours, this very moment. I love you Silas, let me show you how much.'

We do hope that you have enjoyed reading this large print book.

Did you know that all of our titles are available for purchase?

We publish a wide range of high quality large print books including:
Romances, Mysteries, Classics
General Fiction
Non Fiction and Westerns

Special interest titles available in large print are:
The Little Oxford Dictionary
Music Book
Song Book
Hymn Book
Service Book

Also available from us courtesy of Oxford University Press:
Young Readers' Dictionary
(large print edition)
Young Readers' Thesaurus
(large print edition)

For further information or a free brochure, please contact us at:
Ulverscroft Large Print Books Ltd.,
The Green, Bradgate Road, Anstey,
Leicester, LE7 7FU, England.
Tel: (00 44) **0116 236 4325**
Fax: (00 44) **0116 234 0205**

A DISSEMBLER

Fenella-Jane Miller

When Marianne Devenish arrives in Great Bentley she expects to find her great-uncle in residence but instead meets the Earl of Wister, Theodolphus Rickham, pretending to be Sir Theodore Devenish. She is compelled to move in with Lord and Lady Grierson at Frating Hall. But what is their mysterious connection to the local smugglers? As Theo's dissembling leads to heartbreak, Marianne's tattered reputation forces her to flee. Ostracized by society, she seeks refuge at a small estate in Hertfordshire, but her life turns into a nightmare. Can Theo rescue Marianne before she is lost to him forever?